SPECIAL MESSAGE TO READERS

THE ULVERSCROFT FOUNDATION
(registered UK charity number 264873)

was established in 1972 to provide funds for research, diagnosis and treatment of eye diseases. Examples of major projects funded by the Ulverscroft Foundation are:-

- The Children's Eye Unit at Moorfields Eye Hospital, London
- The Ulverscroft Children's Eye Unit at Great Ormond Street Hospital for Sick Children
- Funding research into eye diseases and treatment at the Department of Ophthalmology, University of Leicester
- The Ulverscroft Vision Research Group, Institute of Child Health
- Twin operating theatres at the Western Ophthalmic Hospital, London
- The Chair of Ophthalmology at the Royal Australian College of Ophthalmologists

You can help further the work of the Foundation by making a donation or leaving a legacy. Every contribution is gratefully received. If you would like to help support the Foundation or require further information, please contact:

THE ULVERSCROFT FOUNDATION
The Green, Bradgate Road, Anstey
Leicester LE7 7FU, England
Tel: (0116) 236 4325

website: www.foundation.ulverscroft.com

PARADISE FOUND

Carrie's first visit to Chatterham House, where her grandparents lived and worked, becomes an unexpected turning point in her life when her relationship with her boyfriend ends disastrously there; but she meets Edward, a handsome employee who shares her interest in the estate's history. When she begins volunteering at the house on weekends, she feels drawn to Edward — but the icily beautiful Portia seems to have a claim on him, and his only explanation is that it's 'complicated'. Will Carrie decide he's worth risking her heart for?

Books by Sarah Purdue
in the Linford Romance Library:

STANDING THE TEST OF TIME
PLANNING FOR LOVE
LOVE'S LANGUAGE
TRUSTING A STRANGER
LOVE UNEXPECTED
PLAYING MUM
THE UNEXPECTED GIFT
FINDING ALICE
LOVE FLYING HIGH
PAWS FOR LOVE
FARMER WANTS A WIFE
RUNNING FROM DANGER
NEVER LET YOU GO

SARAH PURDUE

PARADISE FOUND

Complete and Unabridged

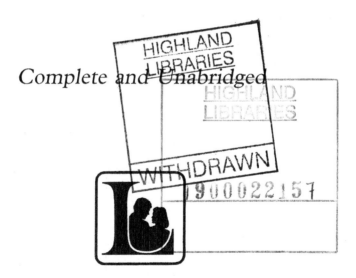

LINFORD
Leicester

First published in Great Britain in 2019

First Linford Edition
published 2019

A catalogue record for this book is available
from the British Library.

ISBN 978–1–4448–4330–9

Published by
F. A. Thorpe (Publishing)
Anstey, Leicestershire

Set by Words & Graphics Ltd.
Anstey, Leicestershire
Printed and bound in Great Britain by
T. J. International Ltd., Padstow, Cornwall

This book is printed on acid-free paper

Stepping Back in Time

Carrie tried to smile. It wasn't easy. She had been looking forward to the visit for years and for some reason Duncan and his mum seemed determined to ruin it.

'Well, I think it's disgusting how much they charge to get into places like this,' Margery said with a disapproving sniff. 'You only have to look around you to see how much money they've got.'

Carrie had to walk away to put some distance between herself and Margery. In truth, she and Margery had never really got along. They were so different and so Carrie had learned to hold her tongue and keep her opinions to herself but today her self-control was being pushed to the limit.

Duncan had known how important this visit was to her, to go back to the place her grandparents had lived and worked during the early years of their marriage, but he had insisted on inviting his mum, and Carrie had known that Margery would be unable to resist the urge to comment negatively on everything.

As they walked through the ground floor of the house, looking at the beautiful rooms full of furniture and walls hung with family portraits, Margery had sniffed and tutted and felt the need to comment on the décor. But to Carrie it was magical.

Her grandparents had told her so many stories of the 'Big House' and she couldn't believe she was finally here and seeing it in person.

Chatterham House, country seat of Lord Cheshire had only opened to the public the year before. Too late, sadly, for her grandparents to return and see their old home. And as much as she tried to screen out the constant nit-picking comments that Margery was making, it was proving to be difficult.

'I don't suppose it's possible to get a

cup of tea around here? No doubt ridiculously expensive,' Margery said as she glared at one of the room stewards, who was too professional to react with anything other than a bland smile and a comment.

'The tearoom is outside in the courtyard, madam, and has a range of home-made cakes to choose from.' The older man bobbed his head slightly and Margery seemed to take this as the first positive thing about the place.

'Right, well let's go straight there, shall we?' Margery said in her usual tone which Carrie knew Duncan would be unable to resist.

'You go,' Carrie said, forcing a smile. 'I'm going to keep looking around.'

Duncan looked between his girlfriend and his mum. He looked at Carrie apologetically.

'I wouldn't mind a cuppa,' he said.

'Go ahead. I'm quite happy to look around on my own,' Carrie said. She silently thought that she was happier without him and his mum.

It was not the first time Carrie had thought this and she wondered if she and Duncan needed to have a serious talk about their future.

It had been amazing at first, as new relationships often were, but as time went on Carrie could see how different they were — and it wasn't the kind of differences that made for a strong relationship.

As she watched Duncan and his mum walk away, she wondered if Duncan felt the same. She shook her head sadly. They would need to talk but today was not the day to do it.

Carrie tried out a smile on the room steward and thought she should probably apologise for Margery. The room steward smiled back with a knowing look in his eyes which told Carrie that Margery wasn't the first person to complain about prices or the décor and she shouldn't worry about it.

'I was wondering . . . ' Carrie started to say. She had wanted to ask someone her question but didn't think she could with Margery around.

Somehow she wasn't sure that she wanted Margery to know how important the place was to her. The older man nodded as if to indicate that she should go on.

'I don't suppose there are any records of the people who worked here?' Carrie bit her lip, expecting the answer to be 'No' but the man smiled broadly.

'We have a whole display down in the kitchens. I can show you if you like?'

'That would be lovely, thank you.' Carrie felt some of the gloom that had settled on her lift a little. Perhaps she would get to experience the place as her grandparents had after all.

The room steward, whose name tag read 'Malcolm', gestured for her to follow him. They headed back out into the grand entrance hall and Malcolm led her through a small door and down a corridor.

'I thought we could take the short-cut. We don't normally allow visitors this way but it's the way the servants would have used and since you seem so interested I thought we could make an exception.'

Carrie's eyes were wide as she tried to take in every feature of the narrow corridor. It wasn't as grand as the rest of the house. It had no family portraits on the wall but somehow to her it was far more important.

'Do you mind me asking why you're so interested?' Malcolm asked, turning briefly to her before moving on down the corridor.

'My grandparents worked here when they were first married. My grandad was a gardener and my grandma worked in the kitchens.'

Malcolm opened a door that led into another corridor but this one was lined with small rooms.

'My father was the butler here until the early nineteen-forties,' Malcolm said as he stopped outside a room which con-tained a small wooden desk and a range of cupboards. 'This was the butler's pantry. I suppose we would call it an office these days. My father used to talk very fondly about taking his supper here with the under butler and the housekeeper.'

Malcolm stepped into the room and Carrie followed him. He showed her some of the account books that his father had handwritten.

'It must be lovely to be able to step back in to his world,' Carrie said softly.

'It is,' Malcolm agreed with a smile which was tinged with sadness. 'I grew up listening to the stories. I was actually born here but my mother and I were evacuated during the war and so I have no real memories of my time here.

'The house was used as an army hospital during the war and then the family was unable to keep the staff on.'

'It's so sad that so many of the old houses were lost that way.'

'It is but Chatterham was luckier than most. George, the youngest son, was too young to fight and so survived the war and managed to keep the estate up and running enough to avoid having to sell up.

'His son Charles is the Lord of the Manor now. The estate was bringing in much-needed funds, but not enough to undertake the considerable repairs to the house after many years of neglect.'

Malcolm and Carrie wandered down the corridor looking into rooms and Carrie felt as though she was having a very personal tour.

'It was Lord Charles who decided to open the house up to the public a few days of the week. Your friend was wrong about the family being fabulously wealthy.'

Carrie could feel herself blush.

'I did try to explain but she saw all the finery and jumped to that conclusion. I'm sorry.'

'Don't be,' Malcolm said with a smile. 'It's clearly not an opinion you share. And I am happy to say that the money raised is helping to restore parts of the house that have been shut up for years. The family actually live in a very small part of it.'

Malcolm led Carrie through an open

door and into the vast kitchen. One wall was lined with a series of black ranges. In the centre was a well-scrubbed wooden table that ran the length of the room. Above it hung all manner of copper pots, pans and jelly moulds.

'This is where your grandmother would have worked. There are food preparation areas and storage areas through there,' Malcolm indicated two doors on the far wall, 'but she would likely have spent most of her time in here.'

Carrie walked up to the long wooden table and ran her hand along it. It seemed that she too was experiencing the ability to step back in time and see things as her beloved grandma would have.

'Malcolm,' a voice said behind Carrie, 'there are some visitors in the servants' quarters who are interested in some of your dad's stories. I don't suppose you would mind . . . ?'

Carrie turned around to see a handsome man, perhaps in his early thirties, with slightly too long brownish hair and a broad grin.

'You know me, Edward — always happy to share.' Malcolm smiled at the younger man.

'Ah — but I can see that you are already engaged,' Edward said, casting his eyes in Carrie's direction.

Carrie didn't know why but she could feel herself blushing.

'Carrie is also a member of the Chatterham 'family'. Her grandfather was a gardener and her grandmother worked in the kitchen.'

'Really?' Edward said and his eyes seemed to light up. 'I don't suppose you would have time to come and look at some photographs with me and perhaps tell me any stories that you remember?'

Edward looked so eager that even if Carrie hadn't wanted to, she knew she would have had to say yes. But as it was, she was so delighted to have an audience who would be interested in her family stories, unlike Duncan and his mum, that she readily agreed.

'I'd love to, if you have time?'

'I have all the time in the world,' Edward said fixing her with his eyes before smiling broadly once more.

'I'm one of the historians for the house,' he added by way of explanation. 'And I'm sure we can rustle up some tea and cake for your trouble.'

Carrie returned the smile. The day had been going downhill so rapidly that she hadn't been able to imagine that it could all change into what she had dreamed it might be.

'That would be lovely,' she said as she fell into step beside Edward and in her mind's eye, she could see her grandad winking at her.

Stop it! She told him silently. He's just interested in what I can tell him about you. A memory of her pops laughing heartily at something she had said started to replay in her mind but she forced herself to listen to what Edward was telling her.

Listening To Mother

Carrie was sitting at a small round table outside Edward's office. It was on the ground floor with access to the large patio that ran along the back of the house.

There were chairs and tables for visitors to bring their refreshments from the tea rooms and the area was comfortably busy. Edward appeared with a tray of tea and cakes and under his arm he had what looked like an old photo album.

'I thought we might need refreshments as we work,' Edward said with a smile. Carrie poured the tea from an old-fashioned teapot and then took the plate of cakes off the tray to make some room on the table.

'We have pretty good records,' Edward said as he took a sip of tea. 'But we aren't always sure who everyone is in the staff photos. Do you think you would be able to point out your grandparents?'

'I might,' Carrie said. 'I have a copy of their wedding photo and they got married whilst they were in service so I should recognise them.'

Carrie wished she had thought to bring the photo with her. It sat in a silver frame on her bedside cabinet and was one of her most precious possessions.

'I've brought the books from the Thirties and Forties. Do you know when your grandparents were working here?'

'My grandad started in nineteen thirty-two. He would have been twelve,' Carrie added, still finding it hard to imagine anyone starting work at such a young age, even though he had insisted he had loved it from the start.

'All that fresh air and greenness, lass,' he used to say. 'After a childhood in the city, it was pure magic!' She smiled as Edward started to turn the pages.

'This is a photo of the gardeners from nineteen thirty-three,' Edward said as they both leaned over to look at the black and white photograph of men and boys in white shirts with the sleeves rolled up and waistcoats, standing in front of the ornamental gardens. Carrie carefully studied each face.

'I think that's him,' Carrie said, pointing to a lanky boy who was grinning like the cat that got the cream.

'That's great. We have a copy of this on the wall in the servants' quarters and I can add your grandad's name.' Edward smiled at her and Carrie got the sense that he was as pleased about all this as she was.

Edward turned the page and they continued to look for more signs of him and then later, her grandmother.

'So typical of Caroline,' the voice said. It was so loud and indignant that Carrie could see the other visitors, who were taking tea on the patio, turn around curiously to look for the source.

Carrie didn't need to look, since she

knew exactly who was speaking and exactly who 'Caroline' was.

'Really, darling, first she drags us to this awful place . . . They had slaves here, you know, slaves!'

'They were servants, Mum, and from what Carrie said, at the time, being a servant was often a good option for the poor. They got three good meals a day and a roof over their heads.'

Carrie felt a slight sense of relief that Duncan was defending her for a change but one glance at Edward and she knew that he was listening to the conversation, even if he wasn't looking in their direction.

'She drags us here and then disappears, so typical of her. When are you going to finish with her and find yourself a decent young lady?'

Carrie could feel the colour rise in her face and could only hope that Edward wouldn't notice. She lowered her head as if to stare more closely at the photographs in front of her and hoped that neither Duncan nor his mother would see her.

'I've told you, Mum. I am going to end it but I couldn't very well do it today, could I? I've told you how important this place is to her.'

Margery snorted.

'If her family worked here then that explains a lot. She's just not the right sort of girl for you, darling.

'For one thing she has no idea how to dress herself and for another, well, I simply don't like her. She's too . . . ' Margery's voice trailed off as she tried to think of a suitable adjective.

'I am going to do it, Mum, but I want to do it somewhere quiet. Somewhere she can't make a scene . . . '

Carrie was sure her face had gone from embarrassed red to furious purple. How dare he? As if she had ever made a scene!

The only time she had ever wanted to was right now. Carrie inched her chair back but felt a hand rest on her arm.

'Why don't we go inside, where it's a little quieter?' Edward suggested kindly.

16

Carrie felt all her anger drain away as she realised that Edward had made the connection between the ghastly conversation and its subject.

Suddenly she felt tears threaten to flow and so she nodded mutely and allowed herself to be led back inside to Edward's office. Edward quietly closed the door behind them, so Carrie didn't have to hear any more of Margery's diatribe.

Carrie walked to the nearest chair and sat in it. She wanted the ground to open up and swallow her.

'I'm so sorry, Carrie,' Edward said and he sounded so genuine that Carrie thought she would lose the battle to hold back her tears. 'I could ask security to see them off the premises?'

Carrie managed a small grin at the thought. When she looked up, Edward's face told her that he was hoping he would at least make her smile.

'Boyfriend?' he asked. Carrie nodded again. 'I know it's not my place but I am positive you can do better and there is one upside.' Carrie looked questioningly at Edward. 'You won't have to put up with his shrew of a mother any more.'

Carrie giggled.

'She is pretty awful,' she admitted.

'A few seconds of listening to her was enough for me.' Edward paused. 'If you don't want to continue I completely understand,' he said kindly.

Carrie shook her head.

'Duncan was right about one thing. Today *is* important to me and I'm certainly not going to let him or his mother ruin it.' Any more than they already have, she added to herself.

'Good,' Edward said, sounding pleased. 'In that case can I suggest that we continue looking at the records and then we find somewhere to have lunch?'

'That would be lovely,' she said. Since she had driven, it wasn't as though Duncan and Margery could leave without her.

Later, she would find them and save Duncan the trouble of telling her it was over. She would tell him and then drive him and his awful mother home and then she would never have to see them again.

But right now she was going to do what she had come to the house to do — find out more about her grandparents' life here.

Edward had left Carrie poring over some old record books, which listed what the servants were paid and what gift they received at Christmas.

The Christmas after her grandparents got married and had been given the right to live in one of the tithed cottages on the estate, their gift had been a bolt of material to make curtains and bedding.

Carrie smiled as she remembered how deft and neat her grandma had been with a sewing needle. She had obviously had plenty of practice.

'Right. I have lunch all sorted and I have the perfect spot picked out.' Edward reappeared in his office.

Carrie jumped to her feet. Edward was being very kind and she had been so absorbed in the history that she had forgotten her manners.

'I'm sorry — I just got a bit carried away.'

'Not a problem,' Edward said. 'It's nice to meet someone who shares my enthusiasm.' He grinned and held the door open for her.

Edward led Carrie through a maze of corridors and then out of a small side door. Parked outside was a small Jeep with *Chatterham House Estates* painted on the side. Edward opened the passenger side door and Carrie climbed in.

'I don't want to get you into any trouble,' Carrie said, feeling that Edward might only be doing what he was doing because he felt sorry for her. She didn't want him to get into trouble with his boss for disappearing.

'You won't. I've spoken to the boss and besides, even servants get to eat lunch.' Edward grinned at her and then put the Jeep into gear.

Daunting Task Ahead

Initially they followed the main road that led from the entrance to the visitors' car park and the house beyond, but Edward took a small turning and before long they were heading off into the estate.

The road turned into a lane and then a dirt track, which they bumped along for some time before Edward pulled to a stop in a small lay-by surrounded by woodlands.

He climbed out and Carrie joined him, as he pulled a picnic hamper and a blanket from the back of the Jeep.

Edward had gone to quite a bit of an effort and Carrie was feeling a little embarrassed. She could only hope it was because they shared an interest in the history of the manor house, rather than that he felt sorry for her after her public humiliation.

'This way,' Edward said and Carrie followed him up a path and into the woods.

They walked for about five minutes in silence, Carrie taking the time to enjoy the peace and quiet of their surroundings and then suddenly they came into a small clearing, which had the remnants of long-forgotten buildings.

'Are these . . . ?' Carrie started to ask, staring from the tumbledown collection of bricks and roof tiles to Edward.

'Yes. Some of the gardeners' cottages. I've been campaigning to get them restored for a while now. But it all costs money, you know?'

Carrie nodded and walked towards the first building, which was in a slightly better state than the others. It still had two standing walls and the space where the window had been.

'Your grandparents lived in number two,' Edward said, holding out his hand to Carrie. Carrie took it, although feeling like she shouldn't. But then the memory of Duncan's hurtful words and those of his mother came flooding back and so she pushed the feelings aside.

'There isn't too much left,' Edward said, interrupting Carrie's thoughts, 'but with a little imagination I think you can see them here.'

Carrie allowed herself to be pulled towards the gap that would have once been the front door. They stepped over the threshold and into what would have been the kitchen and living-room. The walls reached about head height but there was no roof. Carrie could make out what was once the range and part of the chimney.

'It was small by today's standards but I'm told they were fairly cosy. There was plenty of firewood and staff could buy food stuff from the estates at a good price.'

Carrie nodded.

'My grandfather always said it was a good life and that they were well taken care of. He loved it here.' She smiled up at Edward's face. 'He used to tell me all about it. I lived with my grandparents. My father died when I was a baby and so my mum needed help looking after me, so that she could work.'

'I'm sorry to hear that,' Edward said and he seemed to genuinely mean it.

'It was a long time ago. I don't really remember my dad but I had a very happy childhood all the same.'

'I take it your grandparents are no longer with us?' Edward asked the question delicately and Carrie appreciated the fact.

'No, they passed away when I was a teenager. They had my mum very late. They used to call her their favourite surprise. I think they had given up on the idea of having children.' Carrie smiled now as more memories of the happy times she had had, came to mind.

'I'm sure they would be pleased that you have been able to see the estate,' Edward said.

'I know they would love the idea.

Neither of them wanted to leave,' she added sadly.

'Three lots of death duties.' Edward said with a shake of his head. 'It's a miracle really that the youngest son, George, managed to keep the estate going, especially having had to let so many of the staff go.'

'Malcolm told me about it and I remember my grandfather mentioned it once. He didn't talk about leaving here much.'

'Too painful,' Edward said, a comment rather than a question.

Carrie nodded as she stepped through the hole in the wall that would have been the back door.

'My grandad said they had some garden to grow their own vegetables.' Carrie eyed the chest high wall of weeds.

'They did — that's another thing that I plan to put back.'

Carrie turned around. Edward was grinning again and there was a sparkle of excitement in his eyes.

'Why don't we have lunch and I can tell you all about it?' He led the way back through what remained of her grandparents' home to an area which had been cleared.

Edward spread out the blanket and Carrie sat as he pulled a variety of delicious food from the hamper.

'I have managed to arrange some funds so I can at least start the restoration.'

'That's amazing,' Carrie said, helping herself to one of the sandwiches that Edward was offering her.

'My plan is for it to be a living history site. I have the funds to restore the cottages and I plan to have some volunteers on site showing visitors how it was back then.

'You know, allow the children to get dressed up and do a bit of gardening.'

'It's a brilliant idea,' Carrie said and she meant it. She could feel a bubble of excitement of the thought of being able to come back and visit — to see it as it would have been back then.

'Well, I need some volunteers . . . '
Edward said and Carrie could hear the
hope in his voice.

'I'd love to,' Carrie said.

Duncan would have moaned, of
course. No doubt volunteering would
mean all of her free weekends but it
seemed that now she didn't have to
worry about what he thought any more.

Her heart dropped a little. She knew
that breaking up with Duncan was the
right thing, that they weren't right for
each other, but still she knew she was
going to have to give up on the dream
that she had once had.

The dream that they would get
married and have a family. The thing
that she wanted most in her life.

She shook the thoughts away. It
would not have been her dream if she
was with the wrong man.

She needed to focus on something
else for a while and then she could
think about how she could go about
finding the right man.

'I work in the week, of course, but

I'm free at the weekends.' Carrie smiled at Edward. His enthusiasm really was infectious.

'That's perfect. Most of the work will be happening at the weekend — assuming you don't mind helping out with the actual restoration work?'

'Are you kidding? I mean, I don't know much about building but I'm happy to learn and help out where I can.'

'Marvellous,' Edward said, holding up a glass of apple juice. Carrie did the same and they clinked their glasses as if they were drinking fine champagne.

'Here's to the restoration of the past,' he said and Carrie smiled.

When they had eaten their picnic, which was delicious, they sat and chatted. The sun that had been high in the sky when they started, had begun to follow its daily path downwards and Carrie knew that she should be getting back.

After a disastrous start and an acutely embarrassing phase, her day had turned into something more idyllic than she could have imagined but she could still feel the pull of reality and knew that she couldn't leave Duncan and Marjory much longer.

Not only that, but she suspected that Edward had been away from work far too long as it was and she wondered if he felt the pull of the past as she did. He certainly seemed to have enjoyed their time together.

Carrie pushed the thought away. She hadn't even officially broken up with Duncan yet and even when she had, it would be far too early to even think about a new relationship.

No, Edward would be a good friend and she was more in need of that right now than anything else.

'I should be getting back,' Carrie said out loud with great reluctance.

'I should, too, but this spot is kind of magical,' Edward said. 'But I understand. You have some, let's say, unfinished business to sort out?'

Carrie nodded with a small smile.

That was certainly one way of putting it.

'I do, unfortunately, but I will be back when the project starts.'

'Well, I was hoping to start clearing some of the overgrown weeds next weekend. I mean if you're free. I appreciate it's short notice.' Edward seemed to realise he was gabbling and stopped talking, turning his attention to packing up the picnic things.

'I have no plans next weekend,' Carrie said. At least not any more, she thought. 'What time do we start?' Carrie's heart flipped as she saw Edward smile at her.

'Let's say half eight? I usually organise breakfast for the volunteers if we're going to be working hard all day. Just make sure you wear old clothes. I think we're going to get muddy.'

'I'll be here,' Carrie said and together they climbed back into the jeep. Now all Carrie needed to do was tell Duncan that it was over. But despite the fact that she knew it was the right thing, particularly after what she had heard him say, it didn't make the prospect any easier.

A Spanner In The Works

Edward drove the Jeep around the gravel to the front entrance. Carrie could see in the distance that a crowd had gathered.

'Is that for a house tour?' Carrie asked hopefully.

Edward glanced at his watch.

'Can't be. They go on the hour,' Edward said, frowning. He pulled the Jeep up short and climbed out before opening Carrie's door for her.

'Where have you been?' A shrill voice carried over the background murmurings of the crowd and Carrie's heart sank. She would recognise that voice anywhere.

The crowd parted as Margery strode towards her wagging a finger at her as if she were a truculent three-year-old.

'Excuse me?' Carrie managed to say before Edward took a step forward.

'What seems to be the problem, madam? Mrs . . . ?' Edward asked mildly.

Margery looked him up and down in such a condescendingly disapproving way that Carrie thought Edward should follow through on his threat and order security to escort her off the premises.

'Mrs Jones,' Margery said, pulling herself up to her full height of five foot one. 'And I would like to know what you have been doing with my daughter-in-law.'

Carrie stared. Margery could barely bring herself to acknowledge that she was dating Duncan and here she was claiming that they were as good as married. Edward looked from Carrie's shocked face to Margery's furious one.

'I have been showing Carrie where her grandparents used to live,' Edward said but Carrie could tell something had changed in his manner.

Did he actually think that she was engaged — or married — to Duncan and that she had neglected to tell him? That she had lied? By the look on his face that was exactly what he thought.

'I am sorry that I have inconvenienced you, Mrs Jones. Had I known you were waiting I would not have suggested the tour.' Edward did a small sort of bow of the head at Margery and then turned on his heels and left.

All Carrie could do was stare after him as she tried to work out what had just happened. It didn't take her long.

Margery had always seemed to enjoy ruining Carrie's life and even though she wanted her son to break up with Carrie that didn't stop her putting a spanner in the works now.

Carrie glared at her not-mother-in-law.

'I'm leaving. If you want a lift I suggest you come now.'

Since Carrie had never spoken to Margery like that, Margery was momentarily speechless. Carrie took advantage of the pause and walked off in the direction of the car park, aware that the crowd of visitors was now staring after her.

Carrie reached the car and tried to take a deep breath. She had no qualms about ending it now, she had well and truly reached the end of her tether.

'Hey, slow down!' Duncan called as she unlocked the car. 'We've been waiting for you, remember,' he added.

'She never thinks of anyone other than herself, Duncan. I have told you that many times.'

Carrie ignored the latest dig. She felt she ought to be immune to them by now, although Margery was normally more subtle than this.

'Duncan. It's over.' There, she had said it. Duncan's mouth formed an 'O'.

'Wh . . . What?' he asked.

'Oh, don't look so shocked, Duncan. You have wanted to end it for ages. You just didn't have the guts.' Carrie felt suddenly very tired and all she wanted to do was go home and curl up in bed.

'I heard you,' she added, figuring she might as well get it all out in the open, 'as did many other visitors to the estate.'

Duncan looked confused and Carrie couldn't tell if it was an act or if he genuinely didn't know what was going on.

'I was on the patio having tea when I heard what you and your mother said, so I thought I would save you the trouble and just get it over with.'

Duncan stared and Carrie wondered why she had ever thought that they could have a future together.

'We are talking about someone else,' Duncan blustered.

'Really?' Carrie said with a raised eyebrow. 'Let's face it, Dune. We aren't right for each other. You are clearly unhappy. Your mother dislikes me and we both need to move on.'

'Well, it's true I did think we ought to have a little chat . . . '

'And now I have saved you the trouble,' Carrie said, deciding that she didn't want to talk about this any more. She walked round to the driver's side and climbed in.

'Oh, darling, now you see. I tried to

tell you what she was like and now she has gone and broken your heart.' Margery's voice drifted in through the open car window and Carrie laughed.

Trust Margery to make her little boy out to be the victim, forgetting that he had wanted to end it anyway but hadn't been able to rustle up the courage.

Since neither Duncan nor Margery made any move to get into the car as Duncan was too busy being fussed over by his mum, Carrie put the key in the ignition and turned it.

That had the desired effect as Margery pulled open the back door and gestured for Duncan to get inside. For one horrible moment Carrie thought Margery was going to get in the front beside her but instead the older woman walked around the back and climbed in beside her son, relegating Carrie to the role of taxi driver.

No words were spoken on the way home, which Carrie thought was probably a good thing. Some of her anger had died down and all she wanted to do was drop Duncan and Margery at home and say goodbye.

Carrie pulled the car on to the drive of Margery's house which was just a few streets away from Duncan's flat. Margery was out of the car door, practically before Carrie had pulled on the handbrake.

Duncan also climbed out of the car but he leaned down and looked through the front passenger window. Carrie pressed the button that would make the window go down.

'I think we have said all that needs to be said.' Carrie spoke quickly, hoping to cut off any further awkward conversations but Duncan leaned into the car.

'Look, I am sorry about . . . ' Duncan didn't seem to know what to say next.

'Embarrassing me in front of a new friend, allowing your mother to vilify me in public and never thinking to step in and defend me?' Carrie forced herself to stop talking. What was the point?

She would only upset herself and no

doubt Duncan, too. It was over and they both needed to move on. She risked a look at Duncan and he managed to look both hurt and insulted.

'Well, I wouldn't want to get in the way of you and your new 'friend',' Duncan said pointedly.

Carrie sighed.

'I met Edward today and we share a common interest in the history of Chatterham, Duncan.' She said the words slowly as if she was worried that he would have trouble understanding.

'Really, and then you just decided that it was over between us? I don't suppose 'Edward' had anything to do with that decision?' His tone was getting nastier by the second and Carrie wanted to point out that Edward had been nicer to her on one day than Duncan had for months but she held her tongue.

'Duncan, you can think what you want now. It really doesn't matter. I'm sorry that things have ended the way they have but I think we can both agree that it is best if we go our separate ways.'

Carrie put the car into gear as Duncan jumped backwards.

Despite telling herself as she drove home it was the right thing, she couldn't help shedding a tear. The way it had ended should have made her more angry than anything. She had after all put up with a lot from Duncan's mum, but still . . .

It was the end of a nearly two-year relationship and Duncan wasn't all bad. As she parked outside her house, she knew that wasn't the only reason she was crying.

Duncan's words had been hurtful but worse was the look on Edward's face when Margery had described herself as Carrie's 'mother-in-law'. That would be an image that would be difficult to forget.

Close To Home

It was Friday night and Carrie still hadn't worked out what she was going to do. She was desperate to take part in the restoration of the gardeners' cottages but more than that she really wanted to speak to Edward, to explain that what Margery had said was not true. But all she could do was think about the look on Edward's face.

He had looked as if she had betrayed him in some awful way. She had told him that Duncan was her boyfriend, whilst Margery had given a different impression, but still that didn't seem to be reason for him to react in the way he had. Did he think she had lied? Or that she was up to something?

The problem was she didn't know what sort of reception she would receive. Would he even expect her to be there? Carrie still felt fragile after all the hurtful things that Margery and Duncan had said and she wasn't sure she could cope with more rejection.

She walked into her bedroom and picked up the framed photograph of her grandparents on their wedding day. They had looked so happy and so in love. That was part of the problem, Carrie thought, she wanted what they had had, true love. Not perfect but true enough for them to stick together for over 50 years.

Carrie often wondered if it was a fairy tale, if it simply didn't happen in the modern age.

Looking at their faces, Carrie knew she had made up her mind. The cottages were part of her heritage, part of the world that her grandparents had lived and she wanted to help restore them.

Hopefully she would have the chance to speak to Edward and explain. And if he wasn't ready to listen, well then, she wasn't going to let that stop her, either.

★   ★   ★

As Carrie drove up to the side entrance to the expansive parkland she was beginning to question her new found determination. Now she was faced with the reality of seeing Edward again, she was feeling less sure.

She pulled her car into the small drive and a man in uniform stepped out from the small guard hut. He held a clipboard in his hand and walked up to Carrie's car window.

'Morning, miss. Can I take your name?'

'Carrie George,' she said and wondered if this would be the point she would be turned back. What if Edward had taken her name off the list? Carrie's heart was in her mouth for a few seconds as the man flipped over the page, scanning for her name.

'Carrie George? Yes, I've got you right here. I also have a volunteer's temporary ID for you,' the man in uniform said, handing Carrie a paper slip in a plastic cover and then a lanyard.

'You'll need to get your photo taken and an official one sorted in the next few weeks but this should do you for today.' He smiled warmly and Carrie felt herself relax a little. 'Do you know where you are headed?'

'I'm helping with the restoration project on the gardeners' cottages,' Carrie said, returning the smile. Perhaps it was all going to work out fine after all.

'Ah, yes. Edward did mention that you were coming. I understand you had family who worked here?'

Carrie nodded.

'My grandparents.'

'Well, we always like to have family come back and visit. If you follow the road up it will take you to the volunteer and staff car park. If you head to the volunteers' office there should be someone there who can direct you on to the meeting point.'

'Thank you,' Carrie said and made

her way up the long sloping driveway. It looked as if it had been there for centuries and Carrie could almost imagine the horses and carts trundling their way up to the back of the house, laden with goods for the family.

The car park was nearly empty and Carrie figured that the majority of volunteers would arrive later, since the site didn't open for another hour.

There was a small group of people, dressed for outdoor work, standing off to one side and so, feeling a little self-conscious, she wandered over to join them.

'You here to get your hands dirty?' a man of about sixty asked with a grin. He received an elbow in the ribs from a lady of a similar age who Carrie suspected was his wife.

'Trevor! Is that any way to greet a newcomer? This poor lass is just as likely to turn tail and run away with you saying something like that.'

Carrie could tell her comments were half in jest and so she smiled at the woman, thinking, if nothing else, she had found a new friend.

'I'm looking forward to getting stuck in. I'm Carrie,' she said, holding out a hand to the woman.

'I'm Barbara and this is Trevor.'

Carrie shook hands.

'So what brings you out this early on a Saturday morning? A passion for getting muddy?'

Barbara rolled her eyes and smiled at Carrie.

'Actually, my grandparents lived in one of the cottages for a time. So I feel like I have a connection with this place and when I heard from Edward that the cottages were going to be refurbished, I couldn't resist the thought of helping. What about you?'

Barbara and Trevor exchanged glances.

'I wish we had a connection like that,' Barbara said wistfully, 'but we visited when it first opened and fell in love with the place. Since the kids have left home we've been looking for a new project and this seemed like a good place to start.' She smiled at Carrie.

'We get a free lunch, too, and they put on a real spread,' Trevor added and Barbara laughed.

They didn't have a chance to say any more as a figure had appeared and the other volunteers fell silent. Carrie could feel some of her earlier nerves return as she realised that the person was Edward.

When he scanned the small group and his eyes settled on Carrie, she tried to read his expression but her nearest assessment was that he was thoughtful and she wasn't sure if that was a good thing or not.

Carrie was also aware that Barbara was looking at her curiously, but thankfully she decided to keep any comments to herself.

'The vehicles are all loaded with equipment so if you could find a seat in one then we can head off to the site. Today will be mostly clearing the overgrown site but I want everyone to keep their eyes open.

'I suspect we may find all sorts of treasures which have been buried for decades. Anything, however workaday, might help us create a better picture of how the people lived.'

The other volunteers were nodding and climbing into the front and back of some of the estate's old Range Rovers. Trevor climbed into the front seat of one and Barbara in the back.

Carrie waited as long as possible to see if Edward might come over and say hello but he didn't. He just climbed into the driver's seat of the head vehicle and drove off.

Carrie tried to ignore the stab of rejection. Edward was just busy and focused. He had been trying to get the project off the ground for a while and he must be distracted by the fact that today they would finally start work.

Trevor wound down his window.'

'You coming, Carrie, or are you going to stay there all day and admire the view?'

Carrie could feel a blush blossom

and only hoped that meant the view of the manor house as opposed to any connection to Edward.

Barbara opened the car door on her side and slid over so Carrie could climb in. Trevor twisted in his seat to smile at her and she felt a small sense of relief that he seemed oblivious to anything that might be going on between her and Edward.

With Edward in the lead vehicle they followed the same route that Carrie had taken with him before. Carrie couldn't hep wondering what would be worse — being treated by Edward as if they had never met or if he behaved as if he was angry with her.

Barbara, Trevor and the driver kept up a merry banter so at least she didn't feel as if she needed to say anything. The Jeeps pulled up in a row in the lane and everyone climbed out.

'I'm afraid we have to walk from here. The paths are narrow at present, but once we have cleared some of the scrub we are going to put down some shingle so we can get the heavier machinery needed. But for now I'm afraid it's a case of pick up some tools and walk.' Edward was smiling and Carrie could see how excited he was to get started on his pet project. Carrie couldn't help smiling back, it was so infectious.

When Edward's eyes fell on her, she thought this time that his smile dropped a little. She told herself firmly to stop reading things in to the situation that might not even be there.

No, she wouldn't jump to any conclusions, not until she had the opportunity to speak with Edward.

Carrie picked up some long-handled shears and a rake from the back of the Jeep and followed Barbara and Trevor down the path through the woods that would take them to what remained of the gardeners' cottages.

When they arrived Edward was dividing the volunteers into small groups and setting them off to start to cut back the years of overgrown plants and trees. Carrie, Barbara and Trevor set to work hacking back the under-growth around the first cottage.

It was hot, hard work but Carrie was loving every moment. Every small patch they cleared seemed to bring the site a little further back to life and Carrie felt closer to her grandparents than she had for years.

'Right, folks! I think it's time for a coffee. There are bottles of water and cake, which I think we can all agree we have earned.'

* * *

Edward was as pink-faced as Carrie and he was grinning like a child on Christmas Eve.

The volunteers put down their tools and fell on the small table that had been put up and was now laden with supplies. The cakes, a giant Victoria sandwich and a fruitcake, all looked home-made and Carrie's stomach rumbled in antici-pation.

'The lady of the house bakes them,' a voice said next to Carrie. She turned around expecting to see Trevor or one of the other volunteers but the voice belonged to Edward.

'Really?' Carrie managed to say but it came out with a squeak of surprise and part of her wanted to turn away to hide her embarrassment but Edward, for his part, didn't seem to notice.

He was too busy cutting an enormous slice of cake, which he wrapped in a napkin and handed to Carrie.

'I can guarantee that that will be the best cake you have ever tasted.' He grinned and Carrie knew in that moment that all was forgiven and so she grinned back.

'Of course, if your granny worked in the kitchen I suspect that she may have used the same recipe.'

Carrie swallowed down a mouthful of the delicious cake. It was packed with a layer of freshly whipped buttercream and blackcurrant jam. It tasted so much of her childhood that she could feel the emotions rise up and for a moment she thought she might cry.

'By the look on your face, I take it that I'm right?' Edward said and his voice was softer now, as if he could read the range of feelings that Carrie was experiencing.

'You are,' Carrie said. 'My grandma always insisted on blackcurrant jam in her cakes.'

'Mine, too,' Edward replied. 'It's good to see you here. I was a little concerned that you might not come after the events of last week.'

Carrie wasn't sure if he was referring to Duncan and his mother's attempt at public humiliation or his own reaction to Margery's comment, but she wasn't sure it mattered. What mattered was that everything seemed fine between them. Edward seemed genuinely happy to see her and she was here, at the place her grandparents had loved, bringing it back to life.

'Edward, darling.' A young, blonde woman appeared at Edward's elbow and draped a proprietary arm around his shoulders. 'There you are. I've been looking everywhere for you.'

'I can't have been hard to find, Portia, since you knew where I was going to be,' Edward said — a little stiffly, Carrie thought.

Who this new woman was, Carrie had no idea but she seemed to be behaving as if she somehow owned Edward. And why shouldn't she? Edward had never claimed to be single, it was Carrie's own imagination that had taken flight when she had met him.

The best thing she could do right now was leave them to it and get back to work. Maybe work would help her take her mind off the fact that Edward was unavailable.

'I'd best be getting back to work,' Carrie said, forcing a smile.

'But you haven't finished your cake,' Edward said as Portia snorted. Carrie didn't know whether it was because she was eating cake, which clearly someone as thin as Portia never did, or it was the fact that she was working like a gardener.

'I'll finish it later,' Carrie said, turning on the spot and heading back to the first cottage before reaching for a set of hand shears and violently tackling a patch of nettles.

Ridiculous Notion

Carrie knew that she was foolish to feel the way that she did. There were so many factors that made considering starting a new relationship a ridiculous idea.

For starters, she had just finished a relationship which had lasted a little under two years and when it had started, at least, she had thought Duncan might be 'the one'.

That was before she met Edward. She had only met him once but he had been kinder to her on that day than Duncan had ever been. He had also seemed interested in her story but perhaps that had more to do with his job, and not to mention his passion for the history of Chatterham, than anything else?

Of course he had a girlfriend, or maybe she was more than that? Carrie hadn't noticed any ring on his finger but that didn't mean he wasn't married. Lots of men, particularly those who worked outdoors, didn't wear rings.

She swung the rake into a pile of newly felled nettles, feeling cross with herself for behaving like a love-sick teenager.

'Careful, love! You nearly raked up my foot!' Trevor said, taking an exaggerated leap backwards.

'Sorry,' Carrie said, dropping the rake. 'I was distracted.'

'Don't suppose you could be distracted helping me with this waste bag, could you?' Trevor said and he was smiling at her kindly.

'Sure,' Carrie said and held the bag open so that Trevor could shovel in the piles of cut grass and weeds.

'You all right, love?' he asked and Barbara looked up too. Carrie nodded and tried to smile, even though she didn't feel like it at that moment.

'I'm fine,' Carrie said but couldn't avoid the inevitable sigh that followed.

'I was just thinking about life and . . . things.'

'Well, cheer up,' Trevor said, leaning on his shovel. 'You don't want to be ruining a lovely day.' He had his head on one side as if he was waiting for her reaction.

'Trevor, you're quite right. It would be criminal to ruin this lovely day,' Carrie said with a more genuine smile this time.

'It certainly would, lass. Now I think that bag is full enough. Can you grab us another one?'

Trevor was right, of course. Carrie needed to focus on working outside, in glorious sunshine, to help restore something that was important — important to the estate and important to her personally.

There was a lot to look forward to and there was no way she was going to ruin it for herself, by letting her imagination paint a picture of an impossible future with Edward.

★　★　★

When Carrie arrived the next morning, she could feel parts of herself ache in a way they had never done before. She had always thought she was reasonably fit but clearly there were muscles that she had used clearing scrub yesterday that didn't get used in her usual walking and cycling fitness regime.

Carrie was one of the first to arrive and, since there was no sign of Trevor and Barbara, she found a spot on the grass verge beside the car park and flopped down to enjoy the early morning sun.

Yesterday had been a good day, if she could just filter out the bits with Edward and Portia.

Carrie had been careful to sit with Trevor and Barbara when they had stopped for lunch. Picnic blankets had been laid out on the ground and the volunteers had gathered in small groups.

Portia seemed to have decided to

stick around and she had saved a spot for Edward which was well away from Carrie, which, under the circumstances, Carrie had decided was for the best.

She wasn't sure if Edward was actively avoiding her or if Portia was making it impossible for him to come and speak to her again.

'Hello,' a voice said and Carrie drew herself back to the present as she looked up to see a figure in shadow. She lifted up a hand to shield her eyes but still couldn't make out who it was.

'Good morning,' Carrie said in what she hoped was a friendly but non-committal tone.

A car suddenly drew up in the car park and Trevor bounded out.

'Carrie, morning!' he called, striding over. 'Morning, Edward. It was a good day yesterday, wasn't it?' Trevor clapped a hand on Edward's shoulder and Carrie could have sworn that Edward looked disappointed.

'Morning, Carrie,' Barbara said, casting a slightly disapproving glance at her husband who had managed to steer Edward away from Carrie. 'I don't know about you but I'm a tad achy this morning.'

Carrie climbed to her feet and Barbara pulled her into a quick hug.

'Sorry, just so lovely to see you again,' Barbara said, smiling at Carrie as she let her go. 'Good job Trevor didn't see. He's always telling me off for being too 'huggy'.'

'I think the world could probably do with more hugs,' Carrie said, smiling back at her new friend.

'I suspect you're right,' Barbara said as her eyes drifted off to where Edward and Trevor were standing, now deep in conversation.

'You seemed to be having a nice conversation with Edward before Trevor interrupted you,' Barbara said, her eyes not moving from her study of Edward.

'Just saying hello,' Carrie said quickly.

Now Barbara turned to look at her and it was with a knowing smile.

'He is rather lovely, of course,' she

said with a grin playing at her lips.

'He seems very excited about the project,' Carrie said, hoping to steer the conversation to safer ground.

'Aren't we all?' Barbara said with a mischievous twinkle in her eye. Carrie was saved from having to say anything else by Trevor's arrival.

'Apparently it's a smaller crew of volunteers today and so Edward said we can take a Jeep and get started,' Trevor said.

'That sounds good,' Carrie said, thinking that putting some distance between them and Edward would be for the best.

Trevor dangled the keys and Carrie took them before climbing into the driver's seat. Although she had only travelled the route a few times, it all seemed so familiar to her, almost like coming home.

They arrived at the parking spot, gathered up the tools and took the path back to the clearing.

'We've cleared this side of cottage one,' Trevor said, 'so I reckon it's time to go and reclaim their vegetable garden round the back. Who knows what we might find?' He picked up a set of shears and walked around the back of the cottage.

'Fancies himself as a sort of amateur archaeologist,' Barbara said, rolling her eyes.

'Well, Edward did say that we should keep our eyes open for any objects,' Carrie pointed out. 'It's all part of the social history of the place.'

'He did, didn't he?' Barbara said and that twinkle was back in her eye. To avoid any more potentially awkward conversations, Carrie grabbed at some tools and followed Trevor around the back of the cottage.

'Coffee break!' a voice yelled some time later and Carrie stood up, slowly stretching her aching back. 'And there's more cake,' the voice added.

That seemed to galvanise the volunteers into action and soon there was a small queue of people at the pop-up tea table.

'I'm afraid we finished off the Victoria sandwich yesterday but I do have fresh lemon drizzle,' Edward said, smiling. He seemed happy and if he truly wanted her to be his friend then that was all that mattered.

The fact that Portia didn't seem to be his type was nothing to do with her.

'Carrie! Good to see you,' Edward said in what could only be described as an effusive welcome. Carrie could feel herself blush as Barbara looked more than a little amused.

Barbara of course knew that Edward and Carrie had already spoken that morning so the greeting was somewhat unnecessary.

'Hello again,' Carrie said, concentrating on pouring herself a mug of coffee from the urn.

'I was wondering — could we have a quick chat?' Edward asked.

'Sure,' Carrie said. Maybe Edward was going to explain about Portia and the fact that he was already taken. It might be embarrassing but less so if

Carrie could feign an air of polite interest and not give any of her traitorous feelings away.

Lost For Words

Edward walked off towards her grand-parents' old cottage and Carrie followed. She didn't need to look around to know that Barbara was watching them closely.

'Let's go inside, shall we?' Edward suggested which seemed a bit of a grand expression for stepping through the gap in the wall that used to be the front door.

Carrie followed him in through the gap to the back of the cottage which had four walls standing at about eye height. Edward turned around and shifted uncomfortably.

'It's not such a good turnout today but I think we're making good progress,' Carrie said. She thought she should help him out as she didn't like to see him look so uncomfortable.

'We tend to have fewer people on Sundays — other things to do, I suppose,' Edward said distractedly and it was clear this was not what he wanted to talk about.

'True,' Carrie said and they lapsed into awkward silence once more.

'Well, I suppose we had better be getting back to it,' Edward said after the moment of quiet was in danger of stretching into minutes.

'I suppose we should,' Carrie said.

Edward stepped past her and out through the gap in the wall before Carrie could ask him what he wanted to talk to her about. Her curiosity was piqued and so she followed him back outside. As if he heard her steps behind him, he suddenly started talking.

'Right folks, I think it would be good to get back to work. We have a couple of hours before lunch is delivered.' Edward rubbed his hands together and then walked away from Carrie towards the other side of the clearing and all she could do was watch as he disappeared into the woods.

'What was all that about?' Barbara whispered as she sidled up to Carrie.

'I have no idea,' Carrie said, staring at the place where Edward had disappeared from view.

'Don't be coy now,' Barbara said, giving Carrie a little nudge.

'I honestly don't know. All he talked about was how he got fewer volunteers on a Sunday.'

'Well that's obviously not what he wanted to say.' Carrie looked at Barbara. 'It's clear he has a bit of a thing for you,' Barbara added as they went to collect more bags for the green waste. Carrie shrugged.

'I only met him last week.'

Carrie wasn't sure that she wanted to talk about Edward and she knew she didn't want to talk about all that had happened with Duncan either. It was too confusing.

Barbara was right, Carrie was sure that Edward had intended to tell her something else, something more personal, but for some reason he hadn't been able to. It really was like being a teenager again.

She smiled at the thought of Edward getting one of his friends to come and talk to her instead, like Carl Jackson had done when they were fourteen.

The problem was that her relationship with Duncan had some 'teenage' moments and if she was going to take the plunge and start a new relationship then she wanted this one to be different.

She wanted to be able to say what she thought and expect the same from her other half, without the inevitable drama that had been a feature of her time with Duncan.

'Well, to my eyes you've made an impression.'

Carrie smiled. She could point out that Portia seemed to be in the picture but didn't really want to open that can of worms, either. Best to leave it and focus on the work. That had been her plan at the start of the day and it seemed an even better idea now.

'I've got the bags,' Carrie said. 'Do you want to help me fill them?'

Barbara looked as if she was going to say something more but then thought better of it.

It wasn't Portia who delivered the lunch that day and Carrie wasn't surprised. She suspected that Portia wasn't the sort of person who volunteered, not if it meant getting dirty. Carrie felt an immediate flash of guilt. She was making a horrible judgement on a person she barely knew and it was unfair.

It wasn't Portia's fault that Carrie's heart had decided that Edward might be the right man for her. She was so busy mentally telling herself off that she didn't hear Edward approach.

'Carrie, I was wondering if I could have a word.'

'I don't know — can you?' The words were out of Carrie's mouth before she could think about what she was saying. She raised a hand to cover her mouth in case any more thoughts should escape out loud.

Carrie was half aware that Barbara

had sidled away to give them some privacy.

'Sorry,' Carrie said, 'I don't know why I said that.' She looked up hopefully and although Edward looked a bit wrong-footed he didn't seem particularly upset.

'Yes ... about earlier. I didn't actually want to talk to you about volunteer numbers.' He ran a hand through his hair before pulling his Chatterham cap back on.

Carrie waited but Edward seemed to be distracted once more.

'No problem. What did you want to talk about?' Carrie asked, in what she hoped was a brisk and upbeat manner.

'Well, it's about yesterday ... ' Edward started to say but once more his voice trailed off.

'Yesterday?' Carrie echoed, hoping that would be enough to get Edward talking.

'Edward, can you come and have a look at the track we have cleared? I want to know if it is going to be wide enough for the builders' supply truck.' An older man appeared in front of Carrie and Edward and seemed oblivious to the fact that he had interrupted a personal conversation.

'Of course, I'll be right there,' Edward said but the older man just looked at him expectantly and waited where he was. 'Right, well, hopefully I can catch up with you later?' This last comment was directed to Carrie and so she nodded. It seemed that they might be able to catch up but the chances of Edward managing to say whatever he had to say, seemed slim.

'I'd best be getting back to it,' Carrie said as the older man placed a firm hand on Edward's shoulder and steered him away. Edward did look back once and his face was apologetic but Carrie had already headed back to work.

★ ★ ★

Carrie didn't see Edward again until they were packing up. The first few

Jeeps of volunteers had headed off back to the car park but Carrie had said she would stay behind to help clear up the last few remaining piles of rubbish and collect up the tools.

Trevor had offered to stay, too, but Barbara had insisted that they go, saying they had an appointment. When Trevor had asked what appointment, Barbara hadn't been able to come up with an answer and so Carrie was sure that Barbara was making it all up just so that she might have some time alone with Edward.

'Thanks for staying,' Edward said as they tossed the last binliner of cut grass and weeds into the back of the Jeep. 'I could have managed by myself but it's nice to have company.'

'I don't have anywhere else to be.' Carrie said the thought out loud as she imagined her empty flat in the city centre and the Sunday evening that stretched out before her.

Sunday evenings always retained the 'back to school' vibe they had when she was a child and she didn't particularly want to think about work the next day. She would much rather be here in the clearing, which, even though the buildings were in ruin, seemed like a small slice of paradise.

'Me neither,' Edward said but Carrie was sure he probably did. He pulled a small cooler from the back of the Jeep.

'Would you like some apple juice? It's from our orchards on the estate.'

'Lovely,' Carrie said, taking the small bottle and paper straw.

'The estate has been pressing apples for over a hundred years so I'm sure your grandparents would have had some, too.'

Carrie found a spot on a felled tree trunk and Edward came to join her. She smiled. It really did seem an idyllic life. She knew, of course, that it had been hard manual labour and long hours but even that was appealing to Carrie who spent 40 hours a week in an airless office staring at a computer screen. She gave a contented sigh.

'Of all the places on the estate this one seems to draw me every time.'

Carrie smiled.

'You don't fancy being Lord of the Manor and living in the grandeur of the big house?'

Edward gazed at the cottages and for a while Carrie thought that he wasn't going to answer her question.

'Nah, this place is much more me. Can I let you into a secret?'

Carrie felt the breath catch in her throat and she leaned towards Edward so that she was sure she would hear what he would say next.

'I plan to live in one of the cottages when they are finished.'

Carrie blinked. She wasn't sure exactly what she had expected him to say but the idea that he might one day live here was not one of them. Edward turned to look at her.

'You think I'm mad,' he said, shaking his head in a way that suggested he felt no-one understood him. 'Portia says it's ridiculous. The plan is do the cottages up as they would have been pre-war so they will be pretty basic. She just doesn't understand that that is part of the appeal. A simpler life . . . ' Edward stopped talking and looked embarrassed. 'Sorry, I'm rambling.'

'I think it's a wonderful idea. I know some other living history sites that have people living there full time. Obviously they have to put up with people coming into their homes when the site is open and making sure that they don't have anything modern on view but . . . ' Carrie wanted to add that she would love to do that, too, but Edward cut in.

'Exactly. It's perfect. I can live here. I'll make sure there is a locked cupboard for all my personal stuff but other than that, the idea of being away from the internet, my phone and the rest of the world, just seems like . . . '

'Paradise?' Carrie said with a smile. Edward smiled back.

'I knew you would understand. I saw the way you reacted to this place when you first saw it, you understood the magic of it.' Edward shifted so that he was sitting closer to her. Carrie didn't draw away as it seemed the most natural thing in the world.

'I wanted to talk to you about yesterday,' he said softly.

Carrie nodded as her mind raced with what he might have to say and her heart filled with hope.

'It's just . . . ' Edward started to say and then his phone rang. His face crumpled in annoyance and he made no effort to answer it.

'Go ahead. It's fine,' Carrie said, smiling. They had time, she was in no rush and it might be something to do with work. Carrie knew that his work was important to him. Edward grimaced and pulled his phone out of his pocket.

'Hello, Portia? Why are you calling from the house? Yes, I know what I said . . . '

Carrie couldn't hear the words uttered at the other end of the line but she could make out the tone and the tone told her Portia was annoyed.

'Fine. Yes, OK . . . I'll be right there.'
Edward hung up and turned to Carrie.

'I'm really sorry, I have to go but I
can drop you back at the car park.
Maybe we can catch up next week?
Assuming you are free to volunteer.'

'Of course, it's fine. I'll see you next
week.' Carrie forced a smile on her face
but it wasn't easy as she felt her heart
and her hopes had taken another blow.

A Problem Shared

Carrie hadn't been able to focus on anything all week and she knew her boss, the rather formidable Mrs Carter, had noticed. Mrs Carter was like a firm but fair teacher who didn't take any nonsense. She had taken Carrie aside and asked if everything was all right. When Carrie had said she was fine, Mrs Carter had looked unconvinced but reminded Carrie that she had a deadline to meet.

Carrie had forced herself to get the work done and tried to ignore the part of her brain that was setting up a home in her grandparents' cottage on the Chatterham estate.

Edward had made no suggestion that they were considering renting out any of the other cottages once they were restored so she knew it was a pipe dream that could only lead to disappointment.

The problem was she could imagine herself living there and more than that, being happy — a sensation that she felt had eluded her for some time.

When Saturday morning came round she felt a rising sense of excitement. The sort that you get when you are returning to a holiday destination where you have previously had an amazing time. There was overwhelming excitement but a slight reluctance. What if the place had lost some of its charm?

Carrie shook the thought away. She couldn't imagine ever tiring of the little row of cottages, hidden away in the woods that ringed the estate.

She had thought about Edward, too, but the thought of him brought a sense of regret. They seemed to have a connection even her cool head couldn't ignore but the reality was that Edward was not free.

Every time Carrie thought she had cause to hope, Portia seemed to appear on the scene. It now seemed clear to Carrie what Edward had been trying to say and so she made up her mind she would focus on the work, maybe even talk to him about volunteering when the cottages were open to the public but other than that she would keep a polite distance.

In order to avoid having an early morning conversation with Edward, Carrie had decided to arrive just on time.

It wasn't easy since she had a real problem with being late but she had found a little lay-by just a short distance from the staff entrance and had made herself sit and read a book until five minutes before the appointed meeting up time.

When she pulled up into the car park, she was pleased to see it was half full and there was a small crowd of volunteers climbing into the estate Jeeps. Barbara was standing by the door of the last Jeep and waved at her.

'I've saved you a spot,' she said. 'It's busy today.'

Carrie climbed into the back seat and

Barbara got in after her.

'Carrie!' Trevor said. 'We were beginning to think you weren't coming.'

'Just running a bit late,' Carrie said although she was sure she could feel a blush forming at what was not exactly the truth.

The convoy of Jeeps started off in the direction of the lane that would take them to the site.

'I've been dying to talk to you all week,' Barbara whispered, with one eye on Trevor who was in deep conversation with Greg, one of the estate's groundsmen. 'What did Edward want to talk to you about?'

Carrie smiled. Barbara's approach to life was infectious and it was good to know that she had made friends, friends who were interested in her life, even if there were parts of it that she didn't feel ready to share.

'Just about his plans for the site.'

Barbara's smile dropped a little.

'That's all?'

'I don't know,' Carrie found herself

saying. 'I thought he might be about to say something else but then his phone rang.'

'And he answered it?' Barbara said loudly, sounding scandalised. Trevor swivelled round in his seat.

'Who answered what?' Trevor demanded. Barbara made 'go away' motions with her hands.

'I said it was fine. He was at work.'

'Who was?' Trevor asked.

'Someone that Carrie is friends with. You don't know him,' Barbara answered and Trevor turned back around and started talking to Greg again. Carrie made wide eyes at Barbara. The ease with which she had thrown Trevor off the scent was impressive. Barbara just shrugged and Carrie couldn't help a small grin.

'I told him to answer it. I thought it would be about work and I have no right to make demands of him.'

Barbara took a moment to consider this.

'But it wasn't work?'

Carrie shook her head.

'No, it was Portia.'

Barbara's expression suggested that her reaction to meeting Portia had been similar to Carrie's.

'I think they might be together.' Carrie said the words out loud and it was almost a relief to share her thoughts with someone. She could have spoken to friends at work but she just couldn't bring herself to actually start the conversation. But here, Barbara had saved her from having to find a way to broach the subject.

'I'm not so sure,' Barbara said, in a way that suggested she might have insider knowledge. Carrie felt her heart skip but forced herself to remember all that she knew.

'They seem very friendly,' Carrie said sadly.

'Portia seems friendly, Edward seems less convinced.'

'Maybe he just doesn't like public displays of affection,' Carrie said, feeling the weight settle on her chest again. She was beginning to wish she had never said anything. It was a hopeless situation. Did it help to have other people know about it?

'I don't think that's it,' Barbara said thoughtfully. 'You leave it with me and I will see what I can find out.'

Carrie's eyes went wide. The thought of Barbara asking questions about Edward and Portia was not a happy one. What if Edward overheard? What would he think, or say?

'Actually, I think it's probably best if we leave it,' Carrie said hurriedly. 'It's not as if I'm in a position to do anything about it.'

Barbara studied her and Carrie tried to convey her thoughts in her expression.

'And what would that position be?'

'Well I just broke up with my boyfriend,' Carrie said quietly, hoping Trevor and Greg wouldn't hear. She didn't think she could face the inevitable sympathy and support that might follow.

In truth she didn't think she deserved any. It wasn't as if she was heartbroken at the relationship being over. If anything, the overriding emotion was relief.

'Well, I can tell just by looking at you that it was time for the particular relationship to come to an end. Am I right?'

Carrie nodded and wondered how Barbara knew so much. Barbara smiled.

'I have three daughters, love. There is literally nothing I haven't seen when it comes to relationships. When did you end it?'

Carrie wanted to ask how she knew that it was her decision, or at least sort of. Duncan and his mother had certainly helped.

'Weekend before last,' Carrie said.

Barbara nodded.

'And when exactly did you meet Edward?'

'Weekend before last,' Carrie said, wincing just a little. When she said it out loud, it certainly sounded as if the two events were connected. 'But it was nothing like that,' Carrie added hurriedly, worried that Barbara might think she was a terrible person who dumped her boyfriend just because she had found someone she liked more.

'I don't think anything of the sort but I know what it is like when a relationship is not going well and then you see how life could be different.'

'You do?'

'You think Trevor was my first boyfriend?' Barbara asked with a wicked smile.

'I wasn't the first but I'm proud to be the last,' Trevor said from the front seat and despite her embarrassment that he had clearly heard at least part of the conversation, Carrie giggled.

This was the sort of relationship that she wanted. The same as her grandparents. She knew that to make a relationship successful you had to work at it, even when you didn't much feel like it.

But when you did, you ended up with

what Barbara and Trevor had, what her grandparents had had. And that had been the problem with Duncan. She couldn't ever imagine their relationship would be like that, however hard they worked.

No Nearer The Truth

Carrie and her friends arrived, parked on the lane and walked up to the site. Edward was already there, having been in the front Jeep, and was waiting for them.

'Good morning,' Edward said, rubbing his hands together, probably at the sight of all the volunteers who had turned up for the day's work. 'As you can see, we achieved a lot last week and so this week we are going to move around to the area behind the cottages.

'When they were built, each cottage had a garden which was to be used for growing vegetables and other food sources so there may be hidden clues as to what life was like back then.

'So look out for shards of pottery, garden tools, anything really. If you find anything please bring it out to the table here at the front and give me a shout.'

Edward's eyes scanned the crowd and then fell on Carrie's. He held her gaze for a moment and then seemed to remember that they weren't alone.

'Right. I suggest we break for coffee about eleven. As always we have some delicious cakes to keep our workers going.' With that, everyone picked up their tools and headed off to work.

Edward had split up the area behind each cottage and Carrie, Trevor and Barbara were tasked with the area behind the second cottage, Carrie's grandparents' cottage.

Carrie couldn't keep from smiling. She had the real feeling that she might discover some little treasures that would connect her with the past.

'I think I've found something,' Barbara said as she collected up handfuls of cut grass and weeds. She dropped everything that was in her hand except for what looked like a piece of pottery. Carrie hurried over, eager to see. It was a brown earthenware and looked as if was the lip to a narrow spouted jug.

'Here,' Barbara said, handing it over to Carrie who held the broken pot in her hand as if it were a diamond.

'I've see jugs like this before. They used to keep ale in them,' Carrie said excitedly.

'More likely cider in these parts,' Trevor said, peering down at the object.

'One for the table, I think,' Barbara said with a smile. 'Why don't you go and show it to Edward?'

'But you found it,' Carrie said and when she looked up she could see that Barbara was rolling her eyes.

'OK,' Carrie said with a shrug as she tried to pretend that speaking to Edward would be no big deal.

Being back at the site and working to reveal the back garden in which her grandparents had grown their fruit and veg seemed to make her bond with the place feel even stronger.

It made the idea of her living here, where they had lived, seem even more special but she forced the thought from her mind. She needed to stop dreaming about impossible futures. It just made the present, her job in the office and her tiny flat, feel more isolated and lonely.

When Carrie arrived at the table she could see that they weren't the first group to find evidence of the past residents. The table was laden with finds — a wooden bucket minus a handle, the metal end of a fork and a shard of china that looked as if it might have once been part of a tea cup. Edward was there with a notebook and hadn't noticed her approach.

'I have something to add to the finds,' Carrie said and Edward looked up a little distractedly.

'Great, if you could put it . . . ' He stopped and smiled. 'Carrie. I didn't realise it was you. What have you found?'

'We think it might have been part of an ale or cider jar,' Carrie said, handing over the fragment but feeling like she didn't want to let it go.

'You're right. It's a cider jar. We still

use a similar design. See here.' He pointed at the rim where the deep brown colour gave way to a mustard colour. Carrie peered at it. 'That's the very edge of the estate logo.' Carrie nodded, she could just see a small lip of an edge. 'Your grandparents must have enjoyed the cider like the rest of the estate. One of the perks of the job, I imagine,' he added with a grin.

'Whereabouts did you find it? I'm trying to keep an accurate map of the finds.' Edward unfolded a large sheet of paper and spread it out on the one end of the table that had no finds on it yet.

Carrie looked at the map and found her bearings.

'Barbara found it, just there,' Carrie said pointing, as Edward wrote a small number on the map and then added a note to his book.

'I know it's only a shard of broken pottery but to me it feels like finding lost treasure,' he said.

'Me too,' Carrie said, smiling back at him. Neither said anything but they both felt that they had a deep understanding of what the place really meant to each of them.

'I wanted to talk to you,' Edward said and Carrie nodded. She didn't want to be the one to interrupt, not now, when Edward looked like he was finally going to tell her what was on his mind.

'It's about Portia.'

Carrie tried to look a little surprised and only mildly interested but she wasn't sure that she was that successful. Not that Edward was looking at her anyway. He was looking anywhere but in her direction.

'Portia?' Carrie prompted and Edward seemed to remember that she was still there.

'It's complicated, you see,' he said and Carrie nodded, hoping he was going to elaborate.

'These things often are,' she offered, hoping he would explain.

'I'm glad you understand,' he said and now he did look at her and his expression was so relieved that Carrie smiled, even though she had no idea what 'It's complicated' in this context actually meant.

'Well now that's sorted, I'd best be getting on. I can't be seen to be resting on my laurels.' He grinned and then walked off. All Carrie could do was stare after him and wondered what message he thought he had given her. Whatever he thought it was, it was totally lost on Carrie.

'You were a while,' Barbara said, looking up from her spot on the ground where she was wrestling with some particularly truculent weeds between some cracked paving stones.

'Spill the beans,' she said, not looking at Carrie.

Carrie said nothing. It wasn't as if there were any beans to spill. Barbara looked up.

'Don't tell me he's dating that girl? She's all wrong for him!' Barbara said, pulling off one of her gardening gloves and wiping at her face.

'I don't know. He said it was complicated.'

'What does that mean?'

'I've no idea.'

'Well, did you ask him?'

Carrie shook her head although now Barbara mentioned it she wasn't sure why she hadn't just asked him a straight question.

'No. He seemed to think I got the message and went back to work.'

Barbara shook her head in mock despair.

'If it was left up to the pair of you, you would still be dancing around each other when you are ninety.' Barbara stood up and patted Carrie on the back.

'Look, I know you didn't want me to get involved but I think we have passed the point at which the pair of you will figure this out all by yourselves.'

Carrie couldn't see how Barbara could help but settled for nodding miserably. Nothing could be worse than the not knowing. Was Edward with Portia and if he wasn't . . . ? Carrie refused to let her imagination wander down that particular path.

'But don't make a big thing of it,' she urged. 'I'm being such a teenager about all this, it's embarrassing.'

'What's embarrassing, love, is that you can't even ask the man a straight question.' The words sounded harsh but Barbara was smiling kindly. 'So in order to progress things I will find out for you.' Barbara pulled off her other gardening glove and handed the pair to Carrie.

'You can't go and ask now! It will be too obvious,' Carrie said, sounding to her own ears like a spoilt child. Barbara rolled her eyes.

'I doubt, based on current evidence, that he would even make the connection and if he does? Well, at least he will know that you are interested. It's a win-win, really.'

Carrie couldn't see how any of this could be a win-win but since Barbara had marched off, there wasn't much else she could do about it.

'Are you going to stand there staring,

or help me out here?' Trevor was standing by a pile of woody weeds that needed chopping up to fit into the bag. Carrie hurried over and picked up the loppers and started to chop up the nearest branch, all the while keeping one eye out for Barbara, or worse, Edward.

Barbara didn't return before the shout out for coffee and so Carrie and Trevor headed back to the front of the cottage, where hot coffee and fresh cakes awaited them.

Carrie helped herself to a mug of coffee and a slice of marmalade cake and scanned the small group for any signs of Barbara. A small hand waved at her and beckoned her to follow and so she did, hoping that no-one else was watching.

Barbara had found an out-of-the-way spot underneath a huge beech tree, and when Carrie joined her she was rewarded with a big grin.

'I have good news,' Barbara said. Since Carrie had a mouthful of delicious cake she just raised her eyebrows as an indication that Barbara should continue. Barbara eyes twinkled. 'He and Portia used to be together. It looked like they were going to get married but then something happened.'

'Edward told you this?' Carrie was shocked that Barbara had taken such a direct approach.

'No, silly!' Barbara had the look of someone trying to be patient when the other person simply wasn't getting it.

'I decided that going to the source was probably not going to get me as much information as I could get from Jenny.'

'Who's Jenny?' Carrie asked, thinking that she must have missed something, since the conversation was making no sense.

'The lady who brings the coffee and food.' Barbara tutted as if to say 'keep up' but kept speaking. 'She has worked at the estate since before it opened and so she was able to provide some real insight.'

'And?' Carrie asked as Barbara seemed to have become distracted by her slice of chocolate cake.

'It sounds as if Edward was the one who ended it.'

'If it's over then why is Portia still around?' Carrie asked. After all, she hadn't seen or spoken to Duncan since that weekend.

'Maybe it was amicable?' Barbara said but she, too, looked thoughtful.

'The most important thing is that he is free and available.' Barbara said.

'Maybe,' Carrie said, but she really wasn't so sure.

Tinge Of Sadness

On Sunday morning, Carrie abandoned her plan to arrive just on time and aimed for early. If she was early enough hopefully she could simply explain to Edward that she hadn't understood his comments the day before and perhaps he would then tell her what it was that was so complicated with Portia.

The security man waved her through the gates and she followed the long lane up to the car park. Through the trees she caught glimpses of the great house and the beautifully tended gardens.

The view was stunning but for Carrie it didn't compare to the small clearing, which was getting bigger with each day the volunteers worked, and row of tumbledown cottages.

The only tinge of sadness was that her grandparents would never get to see them restored and once again she allowed herself a moment to imagine living there herself.

Carrie had rolled down the windows in the car to allow the sweet smell of the meadows and grassland on either side to float into the car and that was why she could hear the conversation.

'You promised you would come and see Daddy, Edward. You know how much he depends on you to liven up his Sunday and it's not like you made it last week.'

Carrie could see Portia's face and there was a definite pout to it. She felt embarrassed at hearing what was obviously a private conversation, and so tried to busy herself by opening up the boot of her car and pulling out her work boots, but a part of her was desperate to hear Edward's reply.

'I said I would, Portia, but I want to make sure the volunteers are all set up first.'

'They've been working at it for two weeks now. I'm sure that it can't be that difficult to work out how to clear weeds.'

Carrie raised an eyebrow at this comment but kept her head ducked down, pretending to search for something in the boot.

'This is important to me,' Edward said and Carrie risked a glimpse and saw that he had his hands on his hips. 'And before you say it, it is more than just a job. I know that you don't understand it but there it is. I promised your father I would visit him this afternoon and I will — but not until I have got the volunteers all set up.'

'I really don't know why you have to be so stubborn about this,' Portia said.

There was the noise of a car coming up the drive.

'Look, the volunteers are arriving. I will call you when I'm leaving, OK?'

Carrie didn't hear Portia's reply as the car drew up beside her and two of the volunteers, who Carrie didn't yet know very well, climbed out and wished her a good morning.

As the pair walked over towards Edward, Carrie didn't think she could stay where she was any longer and could only hope that Edward hadn't realised she had been listening in to his conversation.

'Morning,' Edward said directing his comment to all of them but smiling particularly at Carrie. The four stood around and chatted as they waited for the other volunteers to arrive and there was no opportunity for Carrie to speak to Edward alone. Once the whole group had arrived Edward spoke to them all.

'Unfortunately I won't be able to spend the whole day with you today as I have a prior engagement this afternoon. But I will leave you in the capable hands of Jenny, who will ensure that you are kept well fed and watered.' He smiled but Carrie got the distinct impression he would have rather been working hard with them than visiting Portia's dad. 'As a result I'm going to take my own vehicle up to the copse so please follow Jenny.'

Everyone climbed into the estate's Jeeps and Carrie was just about to get into her usual Jeep with Trevor and Barbara when Edward caught her arm.

'Would you mind if I borrow Carrie?' Edward asked, leaning down and speaking to Trevor and Barbara.

'Not at all,' Barbara said with that mischievous sparkle in her eyes that Carrie could only hope Edward hadn't noticed. Really, it did feel like she was back at school some days!

'Would you mind?' Edward said, turning his attention to Carrie.

'Sure,' Carrie said with a shrug and then immediately regretted it when Edward looked a little disappointed at her underwhelming response.

She climbed into the passenger side of Edward's Range Rover which looked as if it was older than she was. Edward climbed into the driver's seat and coaxed the engine to start.

'So, how's life?' Edward asked. Carrie stared at him but his eyes were focused on the lane ahead.

'Good, thanks. How are you?' To Carrie that seemed the only possible answer to that question.

'Good, too, thanks. We're making real progress at the site. I think we should have the majority of the land cleared ahead of schedule then we can start looking at the buildings.'

Carrie nodded. This was all good news but not what she really wanted to talk about.

'It's a shame you can't stay today,' Carrie said before she could chicken out.

'It is. I wish I could stay but I promised to visit an elderly friend and I haven't been for a couple of weeks.'

Since Carrie didn't want to admit to hearing his conversation with Portia, she just nodded and looked out of the window.

'I'd much rather be working on site,' Edward said and Carrie could sense his eyes were on her but she didn't turn around.

'It is a special place,' Carrie said, watching the estate pass by the window.

'It is but that's not the only reason,'

Edward said and Carrie froze as the meaning of the words hit her.

'Oh,' she said but it came out as more of a squeak.

'Look, we're nearly there and past experience has told me that we won't get a chance to speak so I wanted to say . . . ' Carrie's heart missed a beat. 'I wanted to say that I've really enjoyed working with you. It's great to have volunteers who are so enthusiastic.'

Carrie nodded and tried to hide any disappointment she was feeling.

'I love that you have the same personal connection with the place that I have,' Edward said, his face a little flushed but serious.

'I do,' Carrie said. Again, it seemed the only thing to say.

'I hope you will continue to volunteer?' Carrie thought she detected some hope in his voice but she was prepared to believe that it was her imagination playing a cruel trick. Surely this was Edward saying that he wanted to be friends and nothing more?

'Of course,' Carrie said, which was true. 'I want to see the project to the end.' Which of course she did but she wondered how she would cope with being around Edward and simply being friends.

'Good. Excellent,' Edward said and his eyes seemed to light up. Carrie managed to smile and looked back out of the window. It was true that she had never felt like this before, that she cared for him in a way that surprised her, considering how long she had known him.

Surely being friends with Edward was better than not having him in her life at all? If that was to be their future then she ought to start getting used to the idea and to do that she needed to forget about the silly dreams that her mind produced at unwanted moments.

Edward pulled his Range Rover up behind the line of estate Jeeps and they both climbed out.

Carrie was relieved when they entered the clearing and were surrounded by other people, which prevented any further opportunities for conversation. Edward set them all up to their tasks before saying good-bye. Once Edward had left, everyone got to work.

'Well,' Barbara said as they carried their tools to the backyard of cottage number two, 'did you have a cosy little chat?'

Carrie sighed.

'Not really. He told me that he was glad I was volunteering and asked if I planned to continue.'

'And what did you say?'

'I said I wanted to see the project out until it's finished and up and running.' Carrie tried not to sound miserable but was finding it difficult.

'That's excellent,' Barbara said cheerfully. Carrie stopped walking.

'How is any of what I've just told you good news?' Carrie asked.

'It's clear that Edward finds it difficult to tell you how he feels.'

Carrie nodded because she felt it was expected, but deep down she was resigned to the fact that Edward didn't have any feelings for her that he wanted to share.

'You have told him that you are going to keep coming and volunteering and that gives him the time he needs to work up the courage to tell you.'

Carrie didn't feel or look convinced.

'Men, particularly men of his background, have great difficulty in getting the words out. All you need to do, my dear, is be patient.'

Carrie had no idea what background Barbara was referring to. Edward didn't seem so different from her but then in truth, she wasn't great at saying how she felt — at least not out loud, to the person those feelings were directed at.

Maybe Barbara was right. Perhaps all Carrie needed to do was relax and see what happened. It wasn't as though she was in a particular rush to jump into a new relationship, even if that person happened to be perfect for her.

Shock News

Carrie felt she had been patient. She had been volunteering for six weeks and other than the friendly conversations with Edward, Carrie was none the wiser as to how he might feel about her.

There were times when she was sure that he wanted something more and other times when he seemed to be firmly in the 'friendship' camp.

She had tried reminding herself of Barbara's advice that Edward just needed time, but how much time? Was he going to be one of those men who never told her how he felt? It was all so confusing.

Edward had brought some professionals to the site who were experts in building restoration. They were working alongside the volunteers in rebuilding the walls of each cottage, using traditional methods.

It was not a fast process but to Carrie it was completely worth it, as she saw her grandparents' cottage rise back up from the ground as if the clocks had been turned back over 60 years.

The walls were being rebuilt with reclaimed stone and mortared in place. It was painstaking but Carrie was loving every minute of it, even though she was covered in dust and streaks of mortar. The back wall of the cottage was slowly growing skywards.

'Coffee!' a well-spoken voice announced. Carrie recognised it instantly.

'It seems Portia is back to 'help',' Barbara said wryly.

Portia had been coming to the site for the last few weekends, dressed in designer gear and avoiding any jobs that might affect her perfect manicure and Carrie couldn't see why she bothered.

It was clear to everyone that she didn't enjoy being on the site and it might be Carrie's imagination but her sighing presence really brought down the sense of enjoyment for the group.

Portia's presence also seemed to have a deep effect on Edward who became much more stiff and formal and acted as if he wasn't permitted to enjoy the work they were undertaking.

'Hopefully she will just deliver the coffee and go,' Carrie said quietly.

'Somehow I doubt it,' Barbara murmured, 'she seems to have come kitted out.' Barbara nodded her head in Portia's direction and Carrie could see that she had an exquisite gardener's apron on, and the pockets were filled with tools, all of which looked as if they had never been ruined by any actual gardening.

'What does she need all that for?' Carrie asked. 'We're building, not gardening.' Carrie could feel herself colour, wishing she had kept the thought to herself. Barbara was clearly not excited to see Portia either but that didn't mean they had to be unkind about her behind her back.

'Well, the back gardens are pretty clear now and I know that Edward wants to get started laying out the ground work for the vegetable patches. Maybe he's asked Portia to help.'

Carrie nodded and forced herself to think of something nice to say.

'It's good that she's come to help.'

Barbara gave her a funny look as if she knew that Carrie didn't actually mean the words she had said. Carrie shrugged.

'I'm just trying not to be like some of the awful girls I went to school with. You know, who said mean things about you behind your back.'

'Good for you,' Barbara said with an encouraging smile. 'It seems that Portia is a fixture in Edward's life so you might need to get used to her being around.'

Carrie tried to return Barbara's smile but she felt like she had swallowed a bucket full of ice cubes. Barbara was right. Edward and Portia were clearly friends, assuming that there wasn't more to it.

They had had a relationship in the

past and although Edward didn't always look completely comfortable with Portia around, he had taken no steps to discourage her.

Barbara had moved off in search of refreshments and Carrie decided to stay where she was. She was halfway through a course of stone work which wasn't the best place to leave things and besides, suddenly she had lost her appetite.

'I brought you a drink,' Edward said. 'I noticed you weren't coming over to get one yourself.' He held out a mug of coffee with a smile.

'I didn't want to stop mid row,' Carrie said, returning his smile. It always felt different when it was just the two of them, although that didn't happen very often.

'I applaud your commitment but you still need to stop for a drink.'

Carrie pulled off her gloves before taking the mug of steaming coffee.

'Thanks.'

'I also got cake. Victoria sandwich with blackcurrant jam, your favourite.'

Carrie felt a surge of happiness at the thought that Edward had paid that kind of attention to the things she liked. She took the slice, feeling that suddenly her appetite was back.

'Edward, darling, I'm clearing away the coffee things. Can I have your mug?' Portia stepped gingerly through the doorway, which was still without a door and cast a disapproving glance around the room. 'I need to get cleared up so I can get started on laying out the first back garden.'

Edward handed his empty mug to Portia. Portia looked expectantly at Carrie, who took a sip of the hot liquid.

'Carrie will bring her mug out to the van when she's finished.'

Portia looked between Edward and Carrie and Carrie thought she saw her face cloud over for a moment.

'Of course,' Portia said brightly. 'Edward, dear, I will need to borrow you to make sure that we are laying out the back garden in line with your plans,' she said as she moved away.

'I'll catch up with you later, Carrie,' Edward said and Carrie nodded, watching Edward follow Portia out of the cottage.

She sighed and took a sip of coffee before putting it on the ground and pulling on her gloves.

She just couldn't work out what Edward was about and there was a small part of her that was telling her that it was a fruitless mission to try to understand him.

An hour later and Trevor and Carrie had swapped roles. Now it was Carrie's turn to find the right stone and hand it up to Trevor. The wall had grown to the point that Trevor needed a step ladder. Barbara was busy mortaring the wall further down.

They seemed to fall seamlessly into step, sometimes chatting and sometimes working in companionable silence and Carrie wished that she could do this for a living. It was certainly much more fun than working in an office.

'Edward has asked for you to come

and speak to him, Caroline,' Portia said. All three of the workers jumped a little, at the unexpected interruption.

'Sorry?' Carrie said, trying to find some composure and wondering who had told Portia what her full name was — the full name that no-one ever used.

'I said, Edward is asking to speak to you.' Portia said the words deliberately slowly as if she couldn't face the prospect of having to repeat herself again to a person who couldn't understand a simple request.

'I'll help Trevor until you get back,' Barbara said, taking the stone that Carrie was still holding in her hand.

Portia had walked to the doorway and Carrie had to jog to catch up. When they had crossed the clearing and headed out into the woods, Portia stopped and turned.

'I know what you are up to,' Portia said accusingly.

'I'm sorry?'

'Don't try to deny it. I've seen you with Edward.'

Carrie couldn't imagine what she had seen since she and Edward were rarely alone and when they were, they talked mainly about the site.

'You need to know something,' Portia said, stabbing a finger in Carrie's direction so that Carrie took a small step backwards.

'Edward and I are in a relationship.'

Carrie raised an eyebrow, she couldn't help it. That wasn't what she had heard, but that was gossip. Portia looked slightly uncomfortable.

'We are working our way through a difficult patch.'

Carrie nodded. It didn't seem that it was worth trying to say anything.

'We need to focus on each other and we can't do that with you hanging around like a love-struck teenager.'

Portia's words were so close to her own take on her emotions that Carrie could feel her cheeks colouring.

'Edward and I are just friends,' Carrie said firmly. If Portia was telling the truth, then that was all they would ever be. 'We both want to see this place fully restored, that's all.'

Portia gave Carrie a withering glare.

'This place is just a distraction. It's always the same with him. We hit a bumpy patch and he feels the need to throw himself into his latest project. When things settle down he'll walk away, he always does.'

Portia's words did not match the impression that Carrie had of Edward but then she didn't know him well, and had only really seen him at work. Perhaps Portia was right.

'That would be a shame,' Carrie said. 'He seems to really love this place.'

Portia snorted.

'Like I said, it's just a temporary distraction. He'll tire of it and then we can get our life back on track.'

'But Edward wants to live in one of the cottages.' For a split second Carrie had a feeling that she had just scored a point. The feeling quickly faded when she realised that she might have betrayed Edward's confidence. Perhaps it was a personal dream for him.

'Edward, live here?' Portia was incredulous but there was also a sliver of fear in her voice. 'Why would he do that when he has a whole mansion to live in?'

'Edward lives in the big house?' In her flustered state, Carrie had used the term that the servants had used for the manor house and Portia simply looked down her nose at her, with fake sympathy.

'Where else do you expect Edward to live? He will inherit.'

Carrie's mouth dropped open and now some of the mysteries seemed to make sense. Barbara had said 'men of his background' and at the time Carrie hadn't known what she meant.

Portia seemed to be enjoying the moment immensely and Carrie wasn't able to keep the shock from her face. Why hadn't Edward told her? Why hadn't she worked it out?

Maybe that was why Edward had said it was complicated. If he was to inherit the estate then he would have to marry the right woman. Perhaps that was Edward's way of saying that she, granddaughter of the estate's gardener, could never be the right woman.

Important Discovery

Portia's look was triumphant. She knew that she had achieved what she set out to do. Carrie was torn between dislike for this woman and relief that she had finally been told that Edward didn't simply work on the estate, the estate was his home and one day he would be responsible for all of it and have the title to go with it.

Carrie couldn't believe that she had managed to overlook all the clues or the fact that everyone seemed to know something she didn't.

Portia was staring at her, daring her perhaps to say something.

'Well, are you coming? Edward said that he wanted to speak to you.'

Carrie's feet wouldn't move. A part of her wanted to run, jump in her car and head home but another part felt like she didn't want to give Portia whatever satisfaction that she was clearly deriving from this situation.

'I'm coming,' Carrie managed to say, her voice only wobbling a little. She had wanted to know and now she did. At least she wouldn't feel like she was walking a high wire every time she was around Edward. Now that she knew they could be friends and nothing more, it would be easier, surely? It wasn't as if he had ever made any kind of promise, in fact he had tried to explain — badly of course — but he had tried.

She felt a flash of anger that she wasn't of high enough station to be with him. But then perhaps the woman who Edward dated and eventually married wouldn't be entirely his choice.

This had been the way of things when her grandparents worked at the house. It wasn't just the servants who were restricted to their class, but the lords and ladies, too. Was there any point railing against a system that had been in place for centuries?

Carrie didn't have a chance to think further as Portia had led her to Edward. He was crouched down looking at a single layer of old stonework that now peeped through some cleared overgrown brambles.

'Carrie, look what I've found! I think the cottages must have also had their own ice house!'

For a moment, Carrie forgot about everything that had just happened and stepped forward eagerly to see what Edward had found.

'An incredible luxury, but I can't think what else it might have been.' He looked up at Carrie, his eyes alight with excitement and she couldn't help smiling in return.

Ice houses were really for the big house only. The idea that the then lord had ensured that his workers would also be able to keep food for longer was almost unheard of.

'I think we will have to see if we can clear it out so we can get a better look at it. It could be a real draw for visitors to be able to see into it.'

'You don't think it's the manor's ice house?' Carrie asked as the thought occurred to her.

'It's not on any plans I've seen and we have one much nearer the kitchens. It would be impractical.' Edward sounded thoughtful. 'I mean for it to be this far away.'

'Are we really going to stand here and admire a few broken bricks?' Portia said and both Edward and Carrie started, as if they had forgotten she was there.

'It's a massively important part of the site's history, Portia. Grand houses didn't usually lavish this kind of luxury on their staff.'

'Lucky servants,' Portia said in that supremely dismissive tone that she had.

Edward ignored the comment.

'It's an insight into the life of the staff. It answers some questions as to why people would choose to work here.' He looked at Carrie and she nodded her agreement.

There had been times growing up, when she had wondered why her grandparents would choose to be in service.

But the more she discovered, the more she could see that it was a positive choice and a good life, in comparison to some of the other choices open to the working classes at the time. At least the air and food was fresh and hard work was a given in any case.

'I'll need to get a surveyor in to check the stability of the ground and to draw up a plan of how to restore it safely,' Edward said, sounding as if he were talking to himself.

'Good idea,' Portia said. 'Shall we go back to the house and call him?' she added hopefully.

'I can do that this evening,' Edward said, 'but I will get some tape and mark out the area. We don't want anyone accidentally falling into the opening.' Edward stood up from his inspection and wiped his hands on his jeans. Out of the corner of her eye, Carrie could see Portia tut with disapproval.

'I'd best be getting back,' Carrie said, feeling like she wanted to leave now. 'I've left Trevor and Barbara rather short-handed.'

'What a good idea,' Portia said pointedly but the remark seemed to be lost on Edward who had turned to take one last look at the ice house entrance.

'Of course. I'm sorry to have dragged you away,' Edward murmured.

Carrie opened her mouth to say it was quite all right, that she was as interested in Edward's find as he was, but Portia cast a dark look in her direction and her message was clear.

'I'll see you later then,' Carrie said and turned to walk away.

'Bye,' Edward said distractedly, as if he wasn't concerned one way or the other.

Carrie stumbled along the path, feeling as if the world were tilting on its axis. How had she not guessed who Edward was? The clues were there but she had all but ignored them and now she felt as foolish.

Even Barbara seemed to assume that she knew the truth. But then Barb's source of gossip didn't seem to be particularly up to date on her facts.

Portia and Edward were going through a difficult patch rather than having split up, and from what Portia had said, it was clear that this happened to them from time to time and they would no doubt sort it out.

In a way Portia had done her a favour, even if it didn't feel like it right now. Now that she knew the full picture she could focus on other aspects of her life, rather than mooning over a man who would for ever be out of reach, whether he had an off and on again girlfriend or not.

Working on the site had made her re-evaluate her life. Working in the countryside had made her long to live in it, to feel part of it. It wasn't as if she particularly enjoyed her job.

She had fallen into it after college and hadn't considered how it would feel still to be working there seven years later.

By the time she reached the clearing where the cottages were, Carrie had managed to recover some of her inner poise. Portia's words had been a shock, and she certainly hadn't delivered them kindly, but at least she knew the truth.

If it had been left to Edward, Carrie suspected that she would still be wondering about him in a year's time. Now she could put that behind her and focus on the other things that she wanted in life.

She walked into the now four-walled cottage to see Trevor and Barbara working on the last row of stones, before they hit the height of where the low roof would be.

'Sorry, I've been ages. Edward thinks that the cottages might have had their own ice house. He's found what he thinks are the remains of the entrance off in the woods.' Carrie mainly spoke to try to avoid any awkward questions that might come her way. Barbara turned from the pile of stones at her feet to glance at Carrie.

'Really? I've never heard of servants having their own before.' She seemed genuinely interested and Carrie gave a small sigh of relief.

'He's going to ask a surveyor friend to come and check it if it's safe for us to uncover. You know, structurally.' Carrie realised that she was gabbling but couldn't seem to stop herself.

'Interesting,' Trevor said at the top of the ladder as he placed another stone. 'Is he planning to open it to the viewing public?'

'I think so, if we can make it safe.'

Trevor nodded but concentrated on his task. Barbara handed him up another stone and then flashed a slightly worried look in Carrie's direction.

'I could do with some water,' she said. 'Do you want some, Trev?'

'Probably could do with a bit of rehydration, thanks.'

Barbara led Carrie out of the cottage.

'By the look on your face I can tell there was more to it,' Barbara said softly as they walked to the cooler which contained the water bottles packed in ice.

'Let's just say Portia has enlightened me.'

'Has she now?' Barbara said darkly.

'She and Edward are going through a rough patch but are working through it.'

Barbara raised an eyebrow and Carrie was worried that she would be talked out of the conclusions she had come to by herself.

'You've only got her word for it — and I'm not sure she can be relied upon.' Barbara handed Carrie a bottle of water and Carrie took a sip.

'There's more than that. Edward tried to tell me but I didn't get what he was saying.'

'And I suppose Portia speaks for Edward, does she?'

'Barbara, I appreciate you being so loyal but actually Portia has filled in some of the gaps for me. Edward said that things were complicated and now I know why. As he is going to inherit he has to marry the right person.'

Barbara looked at her and it was clear she didn't understand what Carrie was getting at.

'A person of the right station.'

Barbara laughed and then realising that Carrie was being serious, stopped abruptly.

'You can't be serious? Carrie, it's twenty-eighteen, not eighteen-eighteen. Not even the royal family are burdened with those social rules any more.'

'Well, Edward is and I can accept that.'

Barbara now looked at her as if she had gone completely mad.

'My grandparents were servants for his family, Barbara. You have to admit that would be awkward.'

Barbara shook her head.

'Why? If you ask me, it just means you have a connection to this place,' she waved her hands around her head, 'as he does.'

'We might not agree with it but he tried to tell me nicely. You know, without making it an insult.'

Barbara raised an eyebrow.

'I think you need to tell me exactly what he said.'

Carrie shook her head.

'It's done and I'm fine with it, Barbara. It's actually kind of a relief to understand where he was coming from. Now I can just concentrate on being Edward's friend. I have plenty of other things in my life that I want to focus on, and to change.'

Barbara nodded slowly but it was clear she wasn't 100 percent convinced.

'Well, OK,' Barbara said, 'tell me about the rest of your life, then. You never know — Trevor and I might have some ideas.' She smiled. Carrie smiled back. Everything would be fine. She would sort out the rest of her life and then maybe she could think about looking for romance again.

Caught Red-handed

The next day, they were working back outside in the garden. Edward had decided that the roofs of the cottages needed an expert. Carrie thought that was probably a wise decision. It had been high enough for her on the stepladder laying the last few courses of stones but the roof needed some scaffolding and Carrie wasn't sure she was up for that.

Besides, the back gardens were really starting to take shape. The ground had been dug over and laid out and so they were digging thin trenches to create different vegetable plots and planting fruit trees.

'Moving house and a new job? That's quite a lot to take on all at once,' Trevor said.

'I know but I've been stuck in a rut for a while now and since I've decided I just really want to get on with it.'

'So are you looking to buy or rent?' Barbara asked, using a watering can to fill the next fruit tree hole with water. Trevor tapped the small blackcurrant bush out of its pot and dropped it in the hole. Carrie shovelled in the soil and then trod it down.

'I'd love to buy but if I change jobs I'll need to rent for a while.'

'It will give you a chance to make sure you are happy with where you are, I suppose,' Barbara said.

'Have you thought about working here?' Trevor asked as he picked up the shovel and started to dig the next hole.

'Are you kidding? I would love that,' Carrie said, 'but I don't suppose there are any jobs going.' She had thought about it but hadn't allowed herself to get too excited. Life never worked out so perfectly, did it? And what if it meant working for Edward? Could she handle that?

'Ask Edward. I'm sure he'd be happy to recommend you,' Trevor said, focusing on digging his hole. Carrie and

Barbara exchanged glances. 'Of course I suppose it would depend on what type of job you were after,' Trevor added thoughtfully.

'What if it meant you couldn't volunteer here any more?' Barbara asked, looking a bit taken aback at the idea. 'That would be a real shame.'

'Are you going to stop volunteering?' Edward's voice made Barbara and Carrie jump but Trevor seemed unaffected. Carrie looked up and saw Edward's concerned expression.

If she didn't know that Edward had a future with Portia she would have taken that as a positive sign for their relationship. It was still good, of course, it meant he valued her help and hopefully her friendship but no more than that.

'No,' Carrie said, 'but I am thinking of changing jobs. Volunteering here at the weekends has made me realise that life in an office is not for me.'

'Well, I hope you can continue to help out here. We would really miss you,' Edward said. Carrie nodded, not knowing what to say to that.

'Things look like they are coming on well here. I have more fruit trees on the truck so help yourself when you're ready.' Edward smiled and then walked across to the yard next door, at present only separated by a piece of string that had been used to size out the plots according to an old map of the estate.

Edward continued to move down the row of cottage back gardens and when he was out of sight and hearing distance, Barbara nudged Carrie.

'He would miss you,' she said with a smile.

'He said 'we',' Carrie replied, 'and it doesn't sound like there are any jobs going on the estate.'

'He might not be involved in that side of things, love,' Trevor said. 'You want to look on the website.'

'Maybe I will,' Carrie said, not feeling hopeful. Surely if there were jobs going on the estate Edward would know about them? Or perhaps he just didn't think she would be suitable for any jobs that were going.

She knew she was being unfair, since Edward had not said anything of the sort but it made her determined to look when she got home and if there was something she fancied she was going to apply.

★ ★ ★

Carrie had taken the day off work. She hadn't told her boss that she was going for an interview. She didn't want to do that until she knew she had something else to go to and besides there was no guarantee that she would get it.

It was a strange feeling driving up through the side gate wearing her best suit. Normally she was dressed in her oldest clothes and ready to get dirty but today she had a job interview. It wasn't a job outside, as she had hoped, and it was only part time but Carrie thought it was a good place to start.

The job involved manning the ticket

office at the public entrance to the park and taking her turn giving house tours. It was three days a week which was not ideal but Carrie had some savings that she could dip into in the short term and once she knew her schedule she figured she might be able to find something else to fit around it.

It also only required occasional weekends, so she would still be able to volunteer.

She climbed out of her car and smoothed down the skirt of her suit. She hadn't realised until that first visit that it was possible to fall in love with a place and now that she had, she couldn't imagine anything better than actually working here.

Carrie had spent the week in the run-up to the interview, learning all she could about the history of the house and the estate. The job description said that full training would be given but Carrie didn't think it would hurt to demonstrate her real interest in the place.

She followed the signs to the management offices which were housed in one of the old stable blocks and entered the small reception area. There was a sign on the wall asking candidates to take a seat, which Carrie did, next to an older lady who smiled at her. She smiled back.

'Are you here for a job, pet?' she asked.

Carrie nodded.

'Are you?'

'No, lass, I gave up work a few years back but I'm here for the living history project.'

Carrie didn't have a chance to ask any more questions as a woman in a suit walked down the corridor to the reception area.

'Caroline George?' the woman said, looking from Carrie to the older lady. Carrie stood up.

The lady in the suit shook her outstretched hand and then led her down the corridor. When Carrie walked into the small conference room where she would be interviewed she was relieved that Edward wasn't there.

It was unlikely that he would have much to do with the interviewing of staff, not at her level, but still it made her feel a little less nervous. A man in an estate T-shirt and cargo trousers stood up and shook her hand.

'I'm Martin Grover. I oversee the staffing of the house and Open Days. Please take a seat.'

The time had flown by and Carrie didn't think she had ever been to an interview that she would have regarded as enjoyable but once her nerves had settled and they had begun to talk about the house and the estate, Carrie had been able to answer questions and share some of what she had learned.

'Well this is most unusual but I for one don't need time to consider Carrie as a potential employee,' Martin said and he shared a smile with Gina, the woman in the suit. 'So, Carrie, it would be our pleasure to offer you a job here at Chatterham. I have no doubt in my mind that you will fit right in and besides all that, you clearly have a very strong connection to the place.'

Carrie thought for a moment she was going to cry. She swallowed and tried to retain her composure enough to speak.

'You don't need to give me an answer right now, of course,' Martin said.

'No, I mean, yes!' Carrie shook her head at her clumsy words. 'What I mean is, I would love to accept the job offer.' She grinned. It probably wasn't the done thing in interviews but she couldn't help herself. 'Thank you. I was caught a little off guard there.'

Martin and Gina smiled back at her and Carrie had the real sense that she was coming home.

'How much notice do you need to give on your current employment?' Martin asked, looking down at Carrie's application form which he had in front of him.

'Four weeks,' Carrie said, 'but I can give notice tomorrow, if that helps.' For a moment she thought she had overplayed her eagerness but both Martin and Gina seemed pleased.

'That would be wonderful,' Gina said. 'We're short staffed at the moment.'

'I have some leave to take, too, so I could probably start in three weeks.'

'That would be even better,' Martin said and he stood up with his arm outstretched. 'We look forward to working with you, Carrie.'

Carrie walked out of the offices feeling like she was on cloud nine. For starters she now had a job that she thought she would enjoy getting out of bed for and she also felt her life was finally starting to gain some direction.

She looked at the ticket in her hand. Martin had said she could spend the rest of the day exploring the house and grounds if she had the time. One look at the house and Carrie knew that there was nowhere else she would rather be.

The last and only time she had explored the house it had been marred by the presence of Duncan and his mother. Margery's constant criticism had really taken the shine off things.

Carrie walked up the stone steps to the great front entrance and handed over her ticket. The volunteer looked at it and smiled.

'I see you will be joining us on the staff soon,' the older gentleman said.

'I will,' Carrie said and again she felt like she was grinning like a child at Christmas.

'Welcome to the family,' the older man said with a wink. 'You'll love it here. I love it so much I come and work here and don't even ask to get paid.'

Carrie laughed.

'I've been working on the gardeners' cottages at the weekends for the same reason.'

'Well, you have a good look round. If you have any questions just pop back here and ask me.'

'I will, thank you,' Carrie said as she followed the arrows into the first room off the main entrance hallway. As Carrie stepped into the room, allowing her eyes a moment to adjust to the lower light levels that were present to preserve the centuries old art work, she heard a voice that was all too familiar.

The last thing she wanted was to have to speak to Portia, for that was who it was, and so she scanned the room and dived through a side door that was standing open. As soon as she was through the door, Carrie pulled it to, leaving just a small gap that she could peep through without being seen. She had no idea what Portia was doing here.

She had made it quite clear that she wasn't interested in helping out unless it meant she could spend some time with Edward and even then she hadn't exactly been an enthusiastic worker.

'Can I help you?' a voice sounded from behind her and Carrie spun on the spot. She stared at Edward and he stared back. Carrie looked around the room and it seemed clear that this was not a public access room. For one thing there was a computer on the stylish

1920s desk and for another there was a flat screen TV on a stand, showing what looked to be CCTV images from different points on the estate.

Carrie's eyes went wide as she realised that she was somewhere she shouldn't be.

'I'm so sorry for intruding, the door was open and I was trying to . . . ' Carrie's voice trailed off. She wasn't sure how to tell Edward that she was hiding from his girlfriend.

Like A Terrible Dream

'Trying to . . . ?'

Carrie's heart sank. It was clear that Edward wasn't going to let her get away without explaining why she had suddenly appeared in what appeared to be his private office. By the look on Edward's face, which was a sort of cheeky grin, he was enjoying every moment of it.

'Well, I wanted to have a quiet look round on my own . . . '

'Not that you aren't welcome in my private office any time,' Edward said as his grin broadened, 'but you look as though you are hiding from someone.' His grin slipped a little. 'The ghastly Margery isn't back, is she?'

'No,' Carrie said slowly as Edward got up from his black leather officer chair and walked around his desk. He was looking at her curiously and then stood at the door. He didn't open it any further but glanced through it as Carrie had done. All Carrie could do was hope that in the intervening time, Portia had gone away to do something no doubt more exciting.

'Ah,' Edward said and Carrie knew he had discovered why she was trying to hide. As quietly as he could he closed the door. 'Ah, yes. Portia, bless her, does have that effect on some people.'

Carrie knew she was blushing but what was the point of hiding it? She had just insulted his girlfriend and indirectly she supposed Edward himself.

'Portia has some lovely qualities as well,' Edward added mildly.

Carrie stared at her feet. She felt like such a fool and all she wanted to do was yank open the office door and make a run for it.

'I didn't mean anything by it,' Carrie started to say but knew that it was pointless. Her actions spoke louder than words. She winced as she realised she had no idea how to explain without making the situation worse. She jumped as Edward laughed. It was such a warm and happy sound that she risked a peek in his direction. Surely a laugh like that meant he wasn't angry with her?

'Don't look so worried,' Edward said. 'I have been known to hide in here myself on occasions.' Carrie didn't bother to hide her surprise. 'Don't get me wrong,' he added, 'there really is a good person in there, it's just she can be incredibly single-minded and then she tends to steamroller other people.'

Carrie wasn't sure that was how she would describe Portia but then to be fair, he knew her a lot better than she did.

Although whether he knew that Portia had warned her off, because they were working on their relationship, Carrie wasn't sure, but she suspected not.

For a split second Carrie thought about telling him what Portia had said but immediately dismissed it.

It wasn't her place to get in between the pair and even if she did feel she had the right to, she knew it was a pretty mean tactic to repeat a private conversation, however justified she might feel.

'I'm not sure you've got to see that side of her. She isn't keen on the renovation project and doesn't mind who knows.' Edward was still smiling and so Carrie took that as a sign that Portia's lack of interest was all right with him, perhaps even that he found it adorable.

'She certainly doesn't seem in her element there,' Carrie said. It was the most neutral thing she could think of to say.

'Portia is more of an organiser, you know, telling other people what to do, rather than a 'get your hands dirty' person.'

Carrie nodded and not for the first time wondered how the relationship between Portia and Edward actually worked. She had heard the phrase 'opposites attract' many times but she had never really understood that and Portia and Edward seemed a case in point.

'So you got the job then?' Edward

said and Carrie started. She had almost forgotten about all that.

'You knew I'd applied?' Carrie asked.

Edward nodded.

'I may have put in a good word.'

Carrie wasn't sure how she felt about that and it must have shown on her face.

'Doesn't sound like I needed to. I don't think I've ever heard Martin so impressed with a newcomer's knowledge of this place.'

Carrie relaxed a little. It was sweet of Edward to have put in a good word but she wanted to get the job on her own merits.

'I've asked Martin to give you minimal weekend days and he agreed. He said that since you were prepared to give up your free time and work for nothing that it would be in the estate's best interests.'

Carrie smiled.

'I would like to keep volunteering whenever I can.'

'I'm glad you are coming to work

here, Carrie. It feels like you are a part of the family.'

Carrie nodded, not trusting herself to keep her feelings hidden.

'Well, I'd best let you get back to work,' Carrie said.

'I would arrange to meet you at lunchtime but I'm afraid I have a prior appointment.' He did look as though he would genuinely rather have lunch with her but Carrie wasn't sure if that was just her imagination going into overdrive.

'No problem. I guess I'll see you Saturday?'

'I wouldn't miss it,' Edward said, walking over to the door in the office far wall. 'I expect the coast is clear but why don't you sneak out this way? People don't tend to hang around in the corridor between the Red Room and library.'

Carrie watched as Edward peeked out of the door and looked both ways and then with a nod of his head, indicated that the coast was clear.

'Thanks,' Carrie said with a giggle and disappeared out through the door. She headed in the direction of the library, which was a room that Margery had declared as 'dull and dusty' and so she hadn't had the opportunity to really take in the splendour.

As she walked down the corridor she had the sense that someone was watching her. She risked a quick glance over her shoulder but all she could see were a couple, one of whom was carrying a sleeping baby in a sling, and they were too busy gazing out of the floor to ceiling windows to the gardens beyond to pay her any attention.

★   ★   ★

By one o'clock, Carrie's feet were aching, not helped by the fact that she was wearing her smartest, and therefore most uncomfortable, pair of heels. She longed to take them off and pad around barefoot but she thought that would probably be frowned upon.

She decided to head for the café and buy a sandwich. If she sat outside on the long patio she was sure she could get away with slipping off her shoes for ten minutes.

Carrie found a table for two tucked around the corner of the building. The view was obstructed by a large weeping willow tree but it was cool in the shade and felt almost private, as if this were her house and there were no visitors.

She had brought a cheddar and ale pickle sandwich and bottle of the estate's homegrown apple juice. She was just taking her first bite when she heard voices.

'What was she doing in your private office — that's all I'm asking?' the voice said, which was clearly Portia's. Carrie looked behind her trying to detect where the voice was coming from and also looking for an exit route. This was not a conversation that she particularly wanted to hear. For one thing, it would be embarrassing and for another, she might hear something that she didn't want to.

'For goodness' sake, I've just told you!' Edward sounded exasperated but still Carrie couldn't see them. They didn't appear to be on the patio and when Carrie moved to look cautiously around the side of the building she couldn't see them there, either.

It was only then that she looked up and could see that a window above her head was pushed open. The voices were coming from a room in the house on the upper floor which was reserved for the family and the public had no access to.

'Carrie came for the reception/house host interview and then decided to have another look around the house.'

'You told me that,' Portia's voice sounded icy, 'but you haven't explained how she made her way to your private office.' Portia put so much stress on the world 'private' that Carrie couldn't help rolling her eyes.

'I also told you that I left the door open by mistake and she wandered in.'

'Oh yes, I can just imagine her

accidentally finding herself in your study. You do realise that she is turning into a stalker.'

Carrie had gathered up her lunch and was just about to tiptoe out of earshot but froze when she heard what Portia had said. She knew she shouldn't be listening but now she had to hear what Edward had to say. What if he thought she was stalking him? She shuddered just imagining it.

'Oh, don't be ridiculous, she's just young and enthusiastic about this place.' Carrie felt the colour drain from her face. That was almost as bad as Edward believing she was stalking him.

All she wanted to do was get home, close the door and then she could be mortified in private. She made a grab at her bag, but it was caught around the leg of the metal patio chair. She tugged it and the strap came free but the chair also tilted and went crashing to the ground.

Carrie didn't stop long enough to pick it up or to see if Edward or Portia would look out of the window. It was bad enough that Edward privately thought she was a silly young woman who had overly romanticised her grandparents' life on the estate but to know that she had overheard him say it was just too awful to contemplate.

She forced herself to walk fast and not run, knowing that would only draw unwanted attention and it was only when she reached the shaded footpath that would lead her to the car park that she allowed the tears to flow.

She wasn't sure what was worse, the pain of that kind of rejection or the overwhelming sense of shame and embarrassment.

*   *   *

Arriving home and closing the door behind her, Carrie thought she might have made a huge mistake. She had accepted a job at Chatterham which would mean that she would cross paths with Edward on a regular basis. Right now she had no idea how she would even look him in the eye.

She flopped down on to her sofa and pulled the woollen blanket down and wrapped it around her. With the stress of an interview and finding out that Edward saw her as little more than an over-enthusiastic puppy, she felt exhausted.

All she wanted to do was close her eyes and hope that when she woke up it would all turn out to be nothing more than a terrible dream.

Wise Advice

Carrie needed to talk to someone. She had thought about one of her friends at work but she wasn't sure they would understand.

They had been universally incredulous that she had spent her weekends working to clear the ground around the cottages, not to mention rebuilding them, and then not being paid for her hard work.

Spending Saturday shopping and then going out in the evening, with Sunday to recover, was their style but it wasn't Carrie's.

In fact there was only one person she could really talk to about this, one person who would understand — and that was Barbara. She sent Barbara a text and asked if she would be free to meet her for lunch.

Carrie knew that she needed to make

a decision quickly. She had told Martin that she would give her notice in today but now she wasn't sure what to do and she knew that Barbara would have some sage advice for her.

Carrie had no reply for over an hour but then she had figured that Barbara probably wasn't a slave to her phone like she was. When her phone beeped, thankfully it was a yes and they arranged to meet at a small café not far from the office that Carrie worked in.

Carrie arrived first and found a small table in the courtyard out the back. She had suggested an early lunch to make sure that she wouldn't run into any of the girls from work.

Barbara arrived soon after and Carrie stood up and hugged her friend. They ordered their food, since Carrie would need to get back to work. Carrie was trying to work out how to explain what had happened and how she was going to do that without getting upset, when Barbara spoke.

'So are you going to tell me about the

interview?' Her words were gentle and Carrie suspected that she thought she hadn't been successful.

'It went really well and they offered it to me,' Carrie said, trying to smile but failing miserably.

'Right . . . ' Barbara said and she looked confused. 'You are going to have to help me out here, honey. I thought this was what you wanted?'

'It is, it's like the dream job I never knew I wanted but now I'm not sure I can accept it.'

Barbara nodded slowly in a way that suggested she still had no clue what was going on.

'Except I already have and now I think I am going to have to ring up and say that I can't.' Carrie's words were tumbling out of her mouth now and she was having to work hard not to sob. Barbara reached out and squeezed her hand.

'OK, OK,' she said soothingly. 'Why don't you tell me exactly what happened from the beginning?'

And so Carrie did. She talked and hardly touched her food. She didn't feel hungry and she wanted to tell Barbara all about it before she had to go back to work.

'That doesn't sound like the Edward I know,' Barbara said, giving Carrie's full plate a disapproving glance. 'You need to eat something,' she said, sounding every bit the mother of three girls. 'Fainting because of low blood sugar will not help the situation.'

'Perhaps we don't know Edward at all,' Carrie said, sniffing back a few tears and forcing herself to eat.

'I'm usually a pretty good judge of character and it doesn't fit. Perhaps you misheard?'

Carrie shook her head vigorously. Every word was etched into her memory.

'Maybe he had more to say — you know, to qualify his comments? You did say you left before you could hear any more.'

Carrie had been trying to convince

herself of this but had had no luck. She felt a little better that Barbara thought it was a possibility and that it wasn't just her heart clutching at straws.

'Also he was talking to Portia and she may not bring out the best in him.'

That wasn't a good thought, either.

'But what do I do?' Carrie said, trying not to wail. Barbara fixed her with a hard stare.

'You want this job?'

Carrie nodded.

'Then, sweetheart, you don't let something as trivial as a man stand in your way.'

Carrie blinked at Barbara's strong words as Barbara reached to give her hand another squeeze.

'It's your dream job in your dream place. You take it. Trust me. You will regret not taking it far more than if you do.'

'I'll give in my notice letter when I get back to work. I said I would do it today.' She smiled a little at the thought. 'But what do I do about Edward?'

'You continue to behave normally. If he knows that you overheard he may even come and speak to you and if he doesn't, you remain polite and let him do all the work.'

Carrie nodded. Barbara was making sense of a situation that had kept her awake most of the night.

'How did you get so wise?' Carrie asked.

'I told you,' Barbara said with a smile, 'I have three daughters and, believe me, they have given me plenty of practice. Now you are coming to the estate on Saturday, yes?'

Carrie had thought she might text and say that she wasn't able to come for the weekend but the thought that Barbara and Trevor would be by her side made her feel much more brave.

'I will, but promise me you'll stick close by. I'm not sure I can face Edward on my own just yet.'

'I will be like your shadow,' Barbara said. 'Now if I'm not mistaken it's time for you to get back to work.'

Carrie glanced at her watch and leaped up. She dug around in her bag for her purse but Barbara waved her away.

'Go, I'll get this. My treat.'

When Carrie didn't move Barbara smiled.

'You can get it next time, OK? You don't want it to look like since you're giving in your notice the office rules no longer apply to you.'

Carrie slung her bag over her shoulder and leaned down to kiss Barbara on her cheek.

'Thank you,' she whispered.

'I'll see you Saturday with your head up and ready to take on the world,' Barbara said and Carrie rushed off back to work.

* * *

Carrie had driven to Barbara and Trevor's small bungalow in a nearby village on Saturday morning. Barbara had suggested she might feel more comfortable travelling in with them and Carrie wasn't about to argue.

Trevor made no comment about her arrival and so Carrie imagined that Barbara must have told him at least some of her story. Not that she minded. Trevor had shown her great kindness and she had a feeling that he would feel fiercely protective of her, something she felt in need of right now but also made her wonder if Edward was right, was she just young and over enthusiastic? She shook the thought from her head.

When they arrived at the cottages they could not believe what they were seeing.

'What on earth?' Trevor said as all volunteers had stopped in their tracks. They all stood and stared. Carrie thought one of the older women might be crying and she didn't blame her. She felt like crying herself. It looked as if someone had thrown a party and not the good kind.

There were beer cans and food wrappers everywhere but that was not the worst of it. There was also paint all over the newly rebuilt walls. Slogans and rude words were daubed on every wall that Carrie could see.

'I'm calling the police.' Edward's voice drifted over the crowd of volunteers. 'Best not to touch anything until they arrive.'

'It must have happened last night,' Trevor said to no-one in particular. 'It looks like whoever the numbskulls were, they thought it would be fun to pull the new tiles off the roofs as well.' Trevor pointed and Carrie could see, amongst the general litter, some smashed slates.

'Who would do this?' Barbara asked and she sounded as shocked as Carrie felt.

'I don't know,' Carrie said, putting an arm around her friend's shoulder. 'Hopefully the police will find out.'

'And we aren't going to let this act of brainless damage stop us,' Trevor said and this time he was addressing all of the volunteers. 'We'll fix what we can and what we can't we will rebuild.' There was a murmur of support but everyone seemed too shocked to get completely behind Trevor's words.

'But what if they come back?' Carrie asked and then put a hand to her mouth. She had not meant to share her thoughts out loud.

'We'll set up a rota and make sure that some of us are camped out here every night,' Trevor said firmly. He turned to Edward who had obviously finished speaking to the police and was now staring at the destruction as if he could not quite take it in. 'Assuming that's all right with you, Edward?' Trevor asked.

Edward seemed to remember that he was not alone and shook himself.

'I can't ask you to do that,' Edward said sadly.

'You didn't ask, we volunteered,' Barbara said, sounding much more like her old self.

'It sounds like a good idea but what if they did come back? What then? It is one thing to have buildings damaged but I won't have people put in harm's way.'

'They wouldn't dare,' Barbara said. 'People who do things like this are cowards.' Barbara gestured at the devastation.

'And besides, Trevor and I have a caravan so with your permission will bring it up to the site, then anyone staying will be safe. If they see anything they can just call the police.' Barbara's tone suggested it was a done deal.

Edward was nodding thoughtfully.

'That isn't a bad plan. I may be able to borrow some accommodation myself. If I am going to ask anyone to camp out then I want to be here too. No-one should feel in any way pressured to stay on site but I would like to invite you to, if you are happy to do so.' There were a few nods amongst the volunteers.

'Barbara, when do you think you can get your caravan on site?'

'We'll go back now and get it,' Barbara said.

'Thank you,' Edward said and there was a slight wobble to his voice. He cleared his throat and looked slightly embarrassed.

'I know you are probably all raring to start to sort this mess out,' he added, 'but the police have asked that we not touch anything until they arrive and they are on their way.

'I have coffee and cake in the van so why not have an early coffee break?'

The volunteers all started to move in the direction of the van. Edward stood separately staring at the damage.

It had been Carrie's plan to keep her distance today but she knew that needed to change.

Suspicion

Carrie watched as Edward moved further away from the coffee and muted conversation. He was careful not to cover any ground affected by the night time visitors but she could see his fist clench even though his face remained neutral.

It was hard to look at the destruction of all their hard work and Carrie felt as if the damage had been done to something that was hers. It was both upsetting and painful.

'Edward?' she said softly as she moved to stand next to him. 'I'm so sorry for all of this but we will get back on track.'

Edward said nothing and Carrie wasn't even sure he had heard her.

'Everyone here is committed to that,' she continued. 'Those of us that can will take turns to stay here on the site.

We won't let anything like this happen again.'

Edward turned to her now and for the first time since they arrived he let his emotions show on his face. There was anger, frustration but mainly pain.

Despite all that had happened, she couldn't bear to see him like this.

'Will you stay?' At first Carrie thought she had imagined the words but Edward was looking at her, really looking at her and she knew that he had spoken them.

'Yes,' she said and tried out a small smile. 'I would love to,' she added and then realised what that must sound like. 'I mean, I don't mean that I am glad this has happened or anything . . . ' She added hurriedly and then saw a twinkle of amusement in his eyes and relaxed a little. 'What I mean is I guess I have always dreamed of living here. I think it's my happy place.'

Edward nodded, not taking his eyes off her face and Carrie felt like she should look away but couldn't.

'It's my happy place, too.'

'We will rebuild it and then you can live here permanently,' Carrie said. Now Edward did smile.

'I will,' he said as if he needed to convince himself, and Carrie wondered if Portia had anything to do with the way he had said it. Carrie knew that Portia would never live here but that was up to them to sort out, she reminded herself.

She, Carrie, was Edward's friend, that was all. His words had hurt her, it was true, but now was not the time to study that particular wound.

The sound of a car on the lane made them all turn and shortly two police officers in uniform appeared up the footpath being escorted by one of the estate managers.

Edward nodded at Carrie and then walked over holding out a hand to the two officers. The male officer pulled out a notebook and started to take notes whilst the female officer skirted around the area of damage taking photographs.

Once she had finished she picked up some of the discarded rubbish and placed each item in a separate plastic evidence bag.

Carrie had joined the group of volunteers and made herself a cup of tea as they all stood and watched the police officers at work. Few words were spoken and Carrie guessed that they were all feeling a little shocked.

The police left just as Barbara and Trevor appeared in their car pulling behind them a caravan. Barbara waved as she jumped out of the car and Edward directed them to the best spot for the caravan.

'The good news is we now have some facilities on site if anyone wants to use them,' Barbara said to the crowd as Trevor set about winding down the caravan's legs.

'That's great, Barbara, thank you. I was just telling everyone that the police have cleared us to get back to work. So I think we need to divide up into teams. Geoff has brought us some litter pickers and black bags. So if we could have half of you on that and for the rest we have some paint remover that we want to try on the graffiti.'

Carrie grabbed a binliner and litter picker before pulling on her gloves. She headed straight for the inside of her grandparents' cottage. She didn't think she could bear seeing it look like an unloved rubbish tip any longer. She stabbed at the first fast food wrapper and dumped it in her bag.

The shock had worn off and now all she felt was anger. She could only hope that the police caught whoever did it and punished them. She jabbed at a beer can.

'I know how you feel.' Edward's voice sounded from behind her. 'I hate seeing it like this. I mean it was bad when I first found the place and it was all overgrown but that was nature — this was idiotic destruction.'

'I don't know what would possess a person to do this,' Carrie said, staring at the graffiti which had been sprayed across the kitchen end of the small room. 'What did the police have to say?'

'They were very sympathetic but not overly hopeful of catching the perpetrators.'

'But they took evidence? Surely they can do DNA tests or something?'

'It's a nice idea but unlike the TV shows, in real life you can only do that on serious cases.'

'This is serious!' Carrie said indignantly.

'To us, maybe but it's not the crime of the century to them and no-one actually got hurt.'

Carrie thought plenty of people had been hurt but she guessed since it wasn't physical injury it didn't count.

'The sooner we get cleaned up the sooner we can forget it happened, I guess,' Edward said.

Again Carrie thought the fact they were going to live on-site to prevent it from happening again was probably going to make that more difficult than he imagined.

'We are sorting out a rota,' Barbara said as she walked into the cottage. She stopped talking as she took in the words that had been scrawled on the walls and shook her head.

'That's great,' Edward said. 'I plan to stay most nights but there may be an occasion when I can't. If that is the case we need a minimum of two people on site. I don't want anyone here on their own.'

'I think we can probably manage to cover most nights,' Barbara said looking at the clipboard she was holding in her hand. 'Trevor and I can be fairly flexible since we are retired.'

'And you haven't asked me yet,' Carrie said. 'I can cover the next few weekends and then when I start work it will be the shortest commute I've had in years.' Carrie and Barbara exchanged a smile and Barbara made a note on her clipboard.

'Weekends are when we are struggling a little so that only leaves us with a few gaps.'

'Thanks for all your help with this,' Edward said. 'It really is going above and beyond your role as a volunteer.'

'Nonsense,' Barbara said. 'Things like this,' she gestured to the pile of rubbish that Carrie was working to clear up, 'just make us all more determined. Now we do have a spare bed in the caravan for tonight, or will your caravan be in place?' Barbara said, looking up at Edward.

'I'll go and chase it up now. I'm sure it will be in place before bed. Is there anything you need? I can ask the guys to bring supplies if you need any?'

'We should be fine for tonight. I even found some marshmallows that we can toast, assuming we are OK to have a fire?'

'Sounds good and yes as long as we don't burn down any buildings.' Edward gave a wry smile.

'Trevor was a Scout. I'm sure that was part of his training,' Barbara said, smiling back.

'Right. Well, I'll leave you ladies to it. I don't want anyone to think I'm shirking my work duties.'

'Do you fancy staying tonight, pet?' Barbara asked Carrie with an air of innocence. 'You and Edward seem to have got over your differences.'

'We haven't spoken about any of it,' Carrie said, turning her attention back to picking up litter. 'I didn't seem the right time to bring it up.'

'Ah, well, some things are best left unsaid,' Barbara said. 'And you didn't answer my question. The caravan has two rooms and I've plenty of food. It might be a nice way to end a difficult day. You can always pop home and pick up a few things.'

'On one condition,' Carrie said, thinking it was a much better way to spend a Saturday evening than going home and staring at the TV all night.

If it weren't for the unfortunate events that had led up to it, she thought she would have been much more excited to finally get to 'live' at least near to her grandparents' former home.

Barbara turned up her innocent

expression a notch and Carrie laughed.

'No interfering in the situation with me and Edward. I'm not sure what I'm going to do about what I heard so for now I will settle for polite friendship.'

'Of course!' Barbara said as if she was horrified at the suggestion she would ever interfere.

'I know you'll be tempted but please. We need to be here to protect the site and the last thing Edward needs is more stress.'

'And what about you?'

'What about me?'

'What about the upset you've been through?'

Carrie sighed.

'I'll admit it has been painful but coming here this morning and seeing this made me realise that other things are more important right now. If Edward and I still want to be friends later down the line, then maybe we can have that conversation.'

'Sounds like a plan. I'll let Trev know he needs to set up the other bed.'

'Thanks. I'm not sure I could face going back to an empty flat.'

'Well, now you don't have to. I'm just going to finalise the rota and then I'll bring some of that paint remover and we'll see if we can't do something about that foul language.'

Carrie had left the site with the other volunteers and driven back to her flat. Once inside she had had a quick shower and then packed a bag, found her sleeping bag and had driven back to the site where Trevor had set up a portable barbecue and Barbara was laying up a trestle table.

'Just in time,' Trevor said. 'I wanted to open a beer but Barbara said I had to wait for you.'

Carrie pulled her bag from the boot of her car. Edward had suggested that she drive it to the site rather than leave it in the main staff car park. There was no sign of Edward's truck but a second caravan had mysteriously appeared.

'Edward's not here yet?' Carrie asked, taking the small bottle of French beer that Trevor was offering her.

'He said he had something to check out but that he would be back before nightfall,' Barbara said. 'I offered to delay the barbecue but he said we should go ahead and eat.'

'Do you think it's something to do with whoever did this?' Carrie said, indicating behind her. The litter had all been collected and placed in bin liners but there was a pile of them.

'Don't you think that's an awful lot of rubbish?' she asked, her eyes fixed on the pile. 'I mean for one night? It looks like hundreds of people were here but that would have been noticed, surely?'

Barbara came and stood by her and viewed the pile of bags.

'It is a lot but who can tell with some people?' Carrie was sure that Barbara wasn't getting what she was trying to say.

'What it if is deliberate?'

Barbara snorted.

'I don't think anyone could accidentally drop that much rubbish.'

'No, I mean what if the damage was intended to disrupt the project?'

'Who would want to do that?' Trevor asked as he flipped a row of burgers over.

'I'm not sure but it does all seem a bit strange, don't you think?'

Barbara shrugged.

'I mean, how did they get in here and why try it? They would have had to climb over a six-foot wall. And besides that, how did they even find this place? Even the family had forgotten where it was.'

Both Trevor and Barbara were staring at her now and for a brief second she thought they were going to tell her she was mad or that she had read too many conspiracy theories on the internet.

'But who would be motivated to want to do it?' Edward's voice sounded from the small pathway. Carrie jumped but Barbara and Trevor seemed to have been aware that he was coming.

'I don't know,' Carrie admitted and then a thought struck her.

The only person she had ever come across who was negative about the project was Portia. But if she and Edward were truly working on their relationship why would she do it?

It was true that she didn't like the work but if you cared about someone, as she claimed to care about Edward, you wouldn't go out of your way to hurt them.

'You have thought of someone. I can see it on your face.'

'No, no,' Carrie said hurriedly. 'I was just running through all the people who know about the site but I couldn't think of anyone who would do this.' Whatever Carrie thought, she couldn't tell Edward her suspicions until she had some evidence. If he thought her a silly young woman who had a crush on him, then he might consider her accusation to be pure spite.

The Burning Question

Carrie woke up in the morning with the sun. Despite the fact that they had gone to bed late, having spent the evening sitting around the campfire talking, Carrie felt surprisingly refreshed.

She pulled a sweatshirt over her pyjamas and pushed her feet into her shoes. The door to Trevor and Barbara's bedroom was closed and so she assumed they were still asleep.

There had been no trouble overnight, or at least none that she had heard, and she had slept with her small window open. She crept down the caravan steps and closed the door carefully.

The air outside was fresh and the sun was starting to filter through the trees. There was no sign that Edward was awake and so for once, Carrie had the site to herself.

She shuffled across the clearing to

the cottages. The roofs still needed repairing but they had managed to clear all the rubbish and remove most of the graffiti.

Carrie slipped through the doorway into her grandparents' cottage, and wandered through and out the back doorway into what would have been their garden. Some of the fruit trees the volunteers had planted had been uprooted and they hadn't had time yesterday to do anything about it. Carrie picked up a set of gardening gloves and a trowel and set to work.

It was so peaceful, with only birdsong to keep her company and Carrie felt once more like she had come home. She supposed that other people might feel the same when they visited the homes that their grandparents had always lived in and they had visited frequently from childhood.

Carrie had never had that but still, every day it seemed the cottage felt more like home. She replanted all the fruit trees and pressed them firmly down into the soil, apologising to them as she went for their previous treatment. Her grandad had always said that plants grew better if they were encouraged and it felt a surprisingly natural thing to do.

'I wonder if they'll ever answer you?'

Carrie smiled. She didn't need to turn around to know that Edward had joined her.

'I don't suppose they will but my grandad always said they grow better and the fruit is sweeter if you talk to them.'

'It's good to see things getting back to normal. The builders will be back tomorrow. I rang them yesterday.'

Carrie brushed her hands together to remove the mud that was stuck to her gloves and pulled them off.

'Well, at least we didn't have any visitors last night.' She turned around and saw that Edward was wearing pyjama bottoms and an old T-shirt. His hair was ruffled from sleep and somehow he looked younger. His eyes were serious as he studied the back yard.

'No, but that doesn't mean they won't be back. I'm going to continue to stay here until the cottages are ready and I can move in,' he said.

'Well, hopefully that won't take too long. Despite all this, I think we're making good progress.'

'We are. Do you fancy a coffee?'

Carrie nodded.

'I'll bring it back here. It seems a shame not to enjoy the sunshine.'

Carrie watched him retreat through the cottage and she sat down on the large stone that remained where the back door used to be. It was a good spot to admire her handiwork.

Edward was back before she knew it and handed her a mug before sitting down beside her. It was a bit of a squeeze but companionable all the same.

'I've been thinking . . . ' Edward said as Carrie took her first sip of what she realised must be freshly ground coffee.

'Oh, yes?'

'Well, I was wondering if you would like to . . . ' His voice trailed off as Carrie looked at him. She had no idea what he was going to say but her heartbeat seemed to be pounding in her ears and she was surprised that he couldn't hear it.

'It's just I had no intention of renting out any of the cottages . . . But I was thinking, and there is no pressure involved, if you would consider living in your grandparents' cottage. I mean I completely understand if you don't want to. It's going to be pretty basic . . . ' Edward stopped talking and Carrie could feel him studying her closely, monitoring her reaction.

'I'd love to.' She finally managed to get the words out. If she was honest it was not the thing she hoped for most but it was second on her list of 'most wanted'. She was going to live here, in this slice of paradise.

'I don't want you to feel like you have to say yes,' Edward said seriously, so seriously that Carrie laughed.

'Are you kidding? I have been dreaming about living here but I didn't know how to ask. It seemed so presumptuous and I didn't want to put you in an awkward position having to say no.'

Edward shook his head as if he couldn't quite believe what he was hearing.

'I can't believe how in sync we are about this place,' he said softly. 'Not many people would understand my obsession with it, let alone choose to live here.'

'I guess paradise is a personal thing,' Carrie added equally softly. Now was the time to ask him about himself, to learn more about it. Carrie just had to be brave.

'Why are you obsessed with it? I mean, besides the fact it is a little slice of paradise?'

Edward snorted with laughter.

'You would be surprised how many people ask me that. After all, I live in a great manor house so why would I want to live down here like a servant?' Carrie raised an eyebrow as Edward's cheeks coloured.

'Sorry, I didn't mean it like that.'

'Relax, Edward. It's fine but it is a good question.'

'Would you live in the manor? I mean if you had a choice?' He was watching her again and she knew that this was an important question for him but she also knew that she could only ever answer honestly.

'No,' she said. 'Not that it's not amazing and beautiful,' she added hurriedly. The last thing she wanted to do was insult his family home. Now Edward was laughing at her.

'It's fine, Carrie.' And they both laughed. 'So why would you chose this place over the big house?' Edward asked.

'I don't think I could live with all that splendour, however beautiful it might be. I think I would be permanently worried about breaking something priceless.'

'And?' Edward sipped his coffee and looked a little mischievous as if he knew he were putting her on the spot.

'Don't get mad but it's a little soulless.' Carrie spoke quickly. 'I mean in comparison to here. It's an amazing place to visit but to live? I'm not sure it would be for me.'

Edward nodded as if he were considering her words and stared out at the garden. They had been laughing only moments ago but Carrie was now concerned she had insulted him.

'My thoughts exactly,' he said after what felt like an eternity.

'You agree with me?' Carrie asked incredulously.

'It's funny that surprises you. I've lived here all my life but never really felt like I belonged. I love the manor and I know I am incredibly fortunate but until I discovered these cottages I don't think I had the connection with the place that the rest of my family does.'

'Will you be allowed to live here — I mean once you inherit?'

'I think my father has a good few years in him just yet.' There was a smile tugging at his lips.

'I didn't mean that.' Carrie's eyes went wide with the horror of the idea

Edward might think she thought that. But he laughed and elbowed her.

'I was kidding. And besides when I am Lord of the Manor I will be able to live wherever I choose.'

Carrie raised an eyebrow.

'Well, I will be in charge,' Edward said in a pompous, put-on voice.

Another thought had occurred to Carrie but she again wasn't sure she wanted to say it out loud. What about Portia?

However hard she tried she simply could not imagine her living down here, not even if the cottages were renovated to superior modern standards. She wanted to ask him but couldn't make herself. It was a step too far, and what if he brought up the other elephant in the room? The fact that she had overheard his words, words that neither of them seemed quite ready to discuss.

'My father is not particularly enamoured with the idea but I've talked him round.'

'I'm glad,' Carrie said. 'How will he feel about me living here, too?'

Edward laughed.

'I suspect he will be relieved.'

Carrie looked at him and he laughed some more.

'I think he is worried I'm going to go all crazy off the grid and I suspect he thinks you will be a civilising influence.'

In truth it wasn't Edward's father's opinion that she was worried about. What would Portia make of it all? Carrie finally had her dream job and dream place to live but she had the distinct feeling that Portia could make her life difficult.

'I have to admit I'm surprised. I can't really picture Portia living here.' Carrie said the words so quickly they came out in a jumble and she instantly knew she would regret having said them.

The Whole Story

Edward just sat and stared at her and Carrie knew she had broken the spell. Somehow the magic of the place seemed to recede and she wondered if the next thing that Edward said would be that asking her to live in one of the cottages had been a mistake.

Carrie stared at her feet and wished she could wind back time, if only for a few moments and stop herself mentioning Portia.

'Why would Portia want to live here? It's not exactly her style, in case you hadn't noticed.' Edward smiled, perhaps at the thought of Portia living in a former gardener's cottage or at the fact Carrie had asked such a strange question. Carrie wasn't sure.

'I thought that you two were . . . ' Carrie's voice trailed off and she wished Barbara or Trevor would come and interrupt them — anything to get her out of this awkward conversation.

'We were, we still are, I guess, but it's not what you think.'

Carrie shook her head.

'It doesn't matter what I think, Edward. It's nothing to do with me.'

'It has everything to do with you,' Edward said softly and reached for Carrie's hand. She looked up and her heart thumped as she saw the look on his face.

'Morning, you two. What a fabulous day to be camping.' Trevor's voice seemed to boom out of nowhere. Edward dropped Carrie's hand and they both looked up at Trevor's smiling face. Carrie felt all at sea.

Only moments before she couldn't have thought of anything better than being interrupted but now, now she felt like the universe was playing a cruel trick on her.

'It's going to be a beautiful day and even better knowing that there was no trouble overnight.' Edward stood up but Carrie stayed where she was, not sure if her legs were up to it yet.

'I have a key to the staff changing rooms where we can all get showered if you want?' Edward turned briefly to Carrie and there was a flash of an apology of his face.

Later, she thought, maybe later we can finish this conversation. As if he could read her mind, he gave her a small nod.

'Do you want to get your things together? I can drive us all up there together, if you like?'

Carrie nodded as Trevor spoke.

'Good plan.' He slapped Edward on the shoulder as the pair of them walked away.

They were all sitting down eating breakfast when the volunteers arrived. Almost as one they expressed relief that the site was as they had left it the night before.

Carrie got swept up in the working day and couldn't seem to find an opportunity to speak to Edward alone.

Worse than that, since she had work in the morning, she was going to go back home once they had finished for the day.

'Only three more weeks to go,' Barbara said as she handed Carrie her bag from the caravan. 'You'd be welcome to stay but that would be a bit of a commute.'

'I'd love to stay but you're right, I need to go home.'

'Well, we'll be here next weekend and you're welcome to come back and stay Friday and Saturday night if you like?'

'That would be great.' Carrie grinned.

'And I hear you might be moving here permanently,' Barbara said looking at her friend closely.

'How do you know about that?'

Barbara shrugged.

'Edward might have mentioned it.' She smiled wickedly. 'I think it's a wonderful idea,' she added.

Carrie glared at her friend who looked even more mischievous than usual.

'Well, you know I've always wanted to live in my grandparents' cottage,' Carrie said pointedly.

'Yes, that too,' Barbara said and Carrie rolled her eyes.

'Ah, Carrie, there you are,' Edward said and Carrie got the distinct impression he was making sure that they knew he was there. 'I was wondering if you would be all right to help pack up tonight. It shouldn't take long but most of the other volunteers need to be getting back.'

'Of course,' Carrie answered. After all there was just her soulless flat in its little block waiting for her. She couldn't wait till the cottages would be ready.

'Great. I'm just going to see the Jeeps off and then we can collect up the tools.'

Carrie nodded and Barbara smirked. They both knew it was just a ploy. The volunteers on the whole were sticklers for staying until it was all sorted and so it seemed Edward had given them an early finish. Carrie shook her head at her friend and then walked off, picking up tools as she went.

'Thanks for staying, 'Edward said when he was back, 'I really appreciate the help.'

'Well, I was hoping we might be able to finish the conversation we were having earlier,' Carrie said boldly. She had been practising the words in her head but she still felt her cheeks colour at the fact she had managed to say them out loud.

'Right,' Edward said, sounding as if he had been caught off guard.

'We don't need to if you don't want to. I mean, maybe you said all you wanted to say?'

'Oh for heaven's sake, you two!' Barbara said, appearing in front of them carrying a tray laden with ice-cold lemonade and a plate of biscuits. 'Take the tray, go to your spot and talk.'

Edward wordlessly took the tray looking a bit like a schoolboy who had been told off by his favourite teacher.

'And do me a favour. Try telling each other exactly how you feel, for once?

I'm not sure I can take too much more of this snail-pace romance playing out.' Barbara grinned, gave Carrie a gentle push in the direction of her grand-parents' cottage and then walked off.

'Right . . . ' Edward said.

Carrie smiled and walked through her grandparents' front door and out to the step behind. She was sure this was where Barbara meant, and sat down. Edward handed her the tray and then sat down next to her. They each took a glass and a biscuit, but neither of them ate or drank anything.

'So about what we were talking about earlier . . . ' Edward said, his voice breaking the long silence.

'You said that you and Portia were sort of together,' Carrie prompted. Edward sighed and took a sip of lemonade.

'Yes.'

'You also told me ages ago that it's complicated.'

Edward nodded.

'Look, I know I've been dancing around the subject for months. I was hoping that it would all get resolved but since we're here now I'll tell you the whole story. That is if you want to know?' He turned to Carrie and Carrie nodded.

There was a part of her that didn't want to know, to preserve the magic that they seemed to be sharing when they were in this place but she also knew they could have no future unless they both knew where they stood.

'Portia and I have been dating for a few years. Our families go way back and I think everyone assumed that we would get married.'

Carrie drunk some of her lemonade as her throat had gone suddenly dry and nodded as Edward appeared to be waiting for some acknowledgement of what he had just said.

'So I proposed. I'm not sure that either of us were really sure but it seemed like the thing to do.'

Carrie wasn't sure that she saw engagement in quite the same light but she could almost imagine how the situation could arise. Edward looked out over the back garden.

'It seems that she was less sure than me as she was seeing someone else.'

Carrie's eyes went wide and she reached out to squeeze Edward's hand. He stared down at it and then smiled at her.

'It was a shock but almost a blessing. Think how much worse it would have been if we had actually gone ahead and got married.'

Carrie was with him so far but she couldn't see how that could lead to the situation that Edward now seemed to be in.

'So I broke it off but a few days later Portia's father had a heart attack. It was serious and has left him basically bedridden with heart failure. The doctors say he has months, perhaps a year.' Edward's voice caught in his throat. 'I've have known him all my life and in many ways I am closer to him than my own dad. He was so unwell that we couldn't tell him and well he still believes . . . '

'He still believes that you and Portia are getting married?'

Edward turned to Carrie.

'I am so sorry — I should have explained. I just was hoping that it would get resolved.' Edward pulled his hand free and ran it through his hair. 'I didn't mean that I want anything to happen to Charles.'

He looked so anguished that Carrie threw an arm around his shoulder and nestled her head in to his.

'I know you didn't. You have done a very kind thing for a man you love.'

'Portia begged me not to tell Charles. She begged me and told me that it was only a matter of months before he succumbed and then we could go our separate ways.'

'I understand,' Carrie said softly. 'Really I do.'

'The thing is . . . I'm not sure how much longer I can go on pretending.'

Carrie wanted to ask about the man that Portia had been seeing but she didn't want to make things worse for Edward. But she had her suspicions. From what Portia had said to her, it sounded as if there no longer was another man and she had her sights set firmly back on Edward. Not that she could tell Edward any of that.

'I was trying to do the honourable thing and I thought I could do it and then I met you that day and I knew I wanted my life to start over. Start over with you. I love you, Carrie. I have since the moment I laid eyes on you.' Edward picked up Carrie's hand and tentatively kissed it.

Carrie knew that, however wonderful Edward's declaration was, she had to tell him that she had overheard what he had said to Portia.

'Edward, I overheard you. The day I came for my interview. I was sitting on the patio having a sandwich and I heard what you said. Not much of it. I left as soon as I realised . . . ' Carrie's voice caught in her throat. She wanted to believe what Edward was saying now but she also knew that she needed him to explain the words he had said in the past.

'I thought it was you. I couldn't be sure. You ran away so fast.'

'I need to know why you said what you did,' Carrie said which of course wasn't really what she wanted to know. What she wanted to know was whether he meant those words or not.

'I'm sorry . . . ' Edward started to say.

'Sorry that I heard them or sorry that you said them?' Carrie felt a flash of anger. It had been so painful, so mortifying to hear those words. They had undermined who she thought Edward was and she needed him to fix it. She just wasn't sure that he could.

Take A Chance On Me

'I'm sorry for all of it,' Edward said and he shifted on the doorstep so that he was turned towards her. Carrie couldn't quite bring herself to look at him. Everything seemed to be balanced on this moment and she didn't think she could bear it if Edward's words didn't heal the pain in her heart.

'Carrie, I was an idiot,' Edward said and Carrie's eyes went wide. Somehow she wasn't excepting him to start there. 'I was caught between doing what I thought was the right thing and the feelings I have for you. When Portia challenged me, I lashed out.

'In that moment I wanted the problem to go away and so I said some things that I didn't mean, that I don't believe for a moment. I didn't want to have to deal with Portia and all her drama.'

Carrie nodded, a lump forming in her throat.

'I know that I can't expect you to trust me, not after all that but I am hoping you will be willing to give me an opportunity to earn your trust again. To show you how I feel.'

Carrie stared out at the garden, at the rows of fruit trees and bushes they had planted. Once they were back on track they were going to tackle planting up the vegetable patch.

In her mind's eye she could see her grandparents working on their small plot of land, laughing and enjoying the evening sunshine. Had they ever said words to each other that they didn't mean? She suspected that they had. Carrie knew that people made mistakes and sometimes hurt the ones they were supposed to love.

'I think you need to talk to Portia,' Carrie said. One thing she was sure of — she didn't want to get pulled into the messy situation. 'Can you do that?'

'If you're prepared to give me a

chance I would do anything,' Edward said. 'Even that,' he added with a grimace. 'And I'll talk to Charles, too.'

'You don't need to do that if you don't want to. I understand why you went along with the pretence, I really do, and I would never ask you to hurt someone you care about.'

'Thank you,' Edward said, reaching for her hand and holding it in his own. Carrie wondered if she should tell Edward about what Portia had said to her, about her relationship with Edward just going through a rough patch. She didn't think it was her place but then another thing struck her and she knew she needed the answer, not from Portia but from Edward.

'Edward?'

'Yes?'

'I need to know if my station in life is an issue for you,' Carrie said the words carefully.

'Your what?' Edward looked confused and amused.' Your what in what?'

Carrie sighed. It was embarrassing enough having to ask the question but to explain it made it so much worse.

'You are going to be a lord one day. You'll be inheriting the estate and I need to know if the fact that my grandparents were servants is an issue.'

'Where on earth would you get an idea like that from?'

Carrie winced. There was no way she was going to tell him but then he started nodding as if he had figured it out by himself.

'Portia. How dare she!' Edward stood up. 'I'm going to go and find her and talk to her right now.'

Carrie stood up and rested a hand on his arm.

'Edward, it's not a good idea to go and speak to her whilst you're angry. You may end up saying things you don't mean.'

'Oh, I'll mean them all right. She had no right to talk to you like that!'

'You may not want to hear this but I

think she wants to be with you.'

'She just wants a title,' Edward said dismissively.

'I doubt that it's just that,' Carrie said drily although she was wondering if that was a factor.

'And besides, she cheated.'

'Maybe she regrets that. People make mistakes, you know.'

Edward sagged a little and then looked rueful.

'You're right,' he said and sat back down. 'Are you always right? It's OK if you are — I just want to know up front.' His eyes twinkled.

Carrie giggled and joined him on the doorstep.

'I only wish I were.'

'I'll give her a ring later and arrange to meet up with her this week.' Edward looked at Carrie as if he were checking he had permission.

'That sounds like a good plan.'

'I'm not sure what to do about Charles, though.'

'Maybe that's something else you

need to talk to Portia about,' Carrie said.

'There you go again. Right as usual!'

Edward reached up a hand and brushed a strand of hair from Carrie's face.

'I guess you need to be heading home.'

'I can stay for a bit,' Carrie said. 'I'm happy right here.'

Edward put his arm around her shoulders and she snuggled in for a hug.

★　★　★

By elevenses on Friday morning, Carrie was counting down the hours. She had her car already packed up for the weekend apart from the food which was still in the fridge so as soon as she was free she was going to walk home, have a quick shower and get in the car.

Barbara had texted her to say her bed was made up and ready and Carrie just couldn't wait. Last weekend had been positively magical and she felt like she had been walking on clouds all week.

She was feeling sad to be saying goodbye to her friends at work but she knew with all her heart that it had been the right choice and with another two weeks to go, she wished her life had a fast forward button.

The office clock, which Carrie was sure had been slowed down on purpose, ticked through to half past four and she grabbed her bag, said her goodbyes and practically ran out of the door.

Just under an hour later and she was driving through the staff gates. She drove up the long drive and then headed off down the lane that would take her to where she could park and then make the short walk to the site.

She had packed light but had also been asked to bring some supplies. The carrier bags weighed heavy on her arms as she staggered up the path.

'Carrie! I said to text me and we would come down and help you,' Barbara said, jumping down the caravan steps and running over to her. She took one of the shopping bags from Carrie's hand.

'It's good to see you, too,' Carrie said with a grin. 'Have you missed me?'

'You know I have. We've had different people staying every night, which has been wonderful but it's hard to relax. It's been like having visitors.'

'And now you've got another one.' Barbara tutted.

'You're not a visitor. You're family. And besides, you understand that camping is basic. Some of the other volunteers seemed to be less accustomed.'

Carrie smiled. Camping wasn't for everyone and neither would living in a cottage without all mod cons, she suspected. But it suited her perfectly.

She scanned the site but could see no sign of Edward. She wasn't particularly surprised. He had said that he had hardly managed to get on the site all week, as the rest of his job was getting in the way.

'Edward's not here yet,' Barbara said

with a smile. Carrie had filled her in on all that had happened over the last weekend, 'but he knows you're coming and I'm sure he won't be long.'

'We thought we'd have pizza tonight. Trevor has been working on . . . '

'Don't spoil the surprise, love!' Trevor said, appearing from behind the caravan and wiping his hand on a cloth. Once he was sure that his hands were clean, he pulled Carrie into a bear hug.

'Show Carrie your prize project,' Barbara said, taking Carrie's bag from her shoulder. 'I'll pop this in your room, love. Do you fancy a cup of tea?'

'Please,' Carrie said, feeling the stress of the week start to fade away as if by magic.

Trevor beckoned her to follow him. He was clearly excited. They walked around the back of Edward's caravan and into a small area of brush that had been cleared. Carrie was sure the work was new and suspected that Trevor had been working on the site during the week.

'Ta-da!' Trevor exclaimed, indicating a sort of lumpy clay structure that sat on top of a round of lopsided stones. 'What do you think?'

Carrie wasn't sure how to ask what it was without insulting Trevor.

'Err, it's great.' Carrie said with enthusiasm.

'It's an oven,' Trevor said and elbowed Carrie. 'I could tell that you had no idea.'

'You built a pizza oven?' Carrie wondered what Edward would make of it, since it wasn't exactly in keeping with the period, not to mention country origins of the cottages.

'No, I built a traditional English bread oven, which also happens to be able to cook pizza.'

'Wow!' Carrie exclaimed.

'Edward and I were doing some research and I found what we think were the remains of an oven. The cottages didn't always have ranges and so the folks would have cooked outside. Before your grandparents' time, of course, although they may have continued to use it.

'Apparently some communities had set days when each household could use the oven.'

'How did you know how to make it?' Carrie said, taking a closer look. The fire was already going and smoke and ash was pluming out of the top.

'I Googled it,' Trevor said with a shrug. 'Edward hasn't seen it finished yet. We need to make sure it's good and hot before we trying cooking our pizza. And we need to make sure it doesn't run out of fuel.' Trevor indicated to a pile of twigs which had been bound into small bundles.

'I'll go and get your tea,' Trevor said and turned to move away.

'What about the oven?' Carrie said, worried to be left in charge of something she knew nothing about.

'You'll be fine. Just push in a bundle through the different holes and keep it burning.

'Friday at last. I don't think I have

ever been so glad for the weekend.' Edward's voice sounded from behind her and now Carrie knew the reason for Trevor's hurried departure. Carrie turned away from the pile of twigs. Edward's face was pinched and he looked tired.

'You look like you've had quite a week,' Carrie said, shaking her head. They had a whole weekend of hard work ahead of them but Edward looked like he needed a weekend off. She doubted she would be able to persuade him to do that.

'Work has been crazy. I haven't managed to get to the site all week. The good news is that the police think they have found who broke in and damaged the cottages.'

'Oh?' Carrie asked, feeling as though she was blushing. She had, after all, thought that Portia might have something to do with it but now that seemed both petty and ridiculous.

'A chap that got fired for helping himself to food in the restaurant.

Thought he would teach me a lesson.'

'That's horrible,' Carrie said.

Edward shrugged.

'He's admitted it, he and his friends were drunk when they did it and not really thinking. We have reached an agreement. He's going to repay the costs involved.

Carrie nodded.

'That's good, then. At least we know. Are we still going to camp out?' It was good news that they had found the culprits but she really wanted to stay on site.

'I think we will. We can let the other volunteers off the hook but I suspect Trevor and Barbara might want to stay, too. It is paradise, after all.'

Carrie smiled it him. She would have liked to leave it there but she knew she needed to ask the next question.

'And how did it go with Portia?'

Edward had texted her on Wednesday to say that he was going to meet Portia for a drink on Thursday evening. Carrie hadn't heard from Edward since and she hadn't wanted to ask him.

She imagined it would not have been a comfortable conversation and he probably needed some time to think about it. But now that he was here in front of her, she didn't think she could wait any longer.

Proposal Of Marriage

Edward pulled over a piece of chopped up tree trunk and collapsed on to it.

'That bad?' Carrie said, shoving some more bundles of twigs into the fire and walking over to Edward. Edward looked up at her and then shifted so that Carrie could sit beside him.

Edward sighed.

'She was pretty shocked. I think she really thought that there was a chance that we could sort things out and still get married.'

Carrie said nothing — there was nothing to say. She felt guilty. Perhaps if she had not walked into Edward's life he might have considered it.

'Oh no, don't you do that to yourself. This is not your fault.' He threw an arm around her shoulders and pulled her tight. 'Portia and I were never going to work. We are too different and we clearly want different things. When I discovered that she was seeing someone else it was a relief.

'I know I should have felt upset and angry but those feelings faded really quickly and instead I knew that she had done us both a favour. We would never have been happy.'

Carrie nodded. There was part of her that believed that too but also a part that still felt as if she had done something wrong. Was she as bad as Portia?

After all, Portia had told her that she wanted to get back together with Edward. Carrie had known that. She had tried to keep her distance but her heart had had other ideas.

'Portia will be fine. She just needs some time to adjust,' Edward said, sounding as much like he needed to convince himself as he did Carrie.

'And what about Charles?'

'He is doing better than the doctors ever thought possible but he is very frail.'

Carrie nodded. She could understand the dilemma that Edward was facing and in no way wanted to influence his decision. This had to be his choice and his choice alone.

'Whatever you decide, I support you one hundred percent,' Carrie said, before squeezing his hand.

'Portia wants to carry on with the ruse but I'm not so sure.'

'I can see why she might feel that way.'

Edward looked down at her.

'She wouldn't be so charitable if your situations were reversed.'

'You don't know that,' Carrie said, thinking that Edward was being a little harsh, although he did know Portia better than she did. 'And besides, she's had a lot to deal with lately from the sounds of things.'

Edward blew out a long breath.

'You're right, as always.' He smiled at Carrie in a way that made her feel like her heart was going to melt.

*   *   *

On Sunday morning Edward and Carrie repeated their ritual of drinking their first cup of coffee sitting on the back doorstep of her grandparents' cottage.

'How much longer do you think it will be before the site will be ready?' Carrie asked as she took a sip.

'You mean how much longer before you can move in?' Edward said with a smile.

'That may have been a factor in my question,' Carrie said, smiling out at the garden that she had finished planting out the day before.

'It's going to be basic, you know? No dishwasher, no Wi-Fi, no broadband . . . You'll have to use the office in the main house if you want to send e-mails. You won't get a mobile signal here, either.'

'Perfect, peace and quiet when I'm not working,' Carrie replied. She took another sip of her coffee. 'Are you trying to put me off?' She looked at Edward curiously. He had told her this several times and her replies hadn't changed.

'No, of course not. I just want you to be sure.'

'Well, I am. Unless you've changed your mind? I mean, I'd understand it if you want to keep this place to yourself.'

'I can't imagine anyone else I would want to share it with,' Edward said, pulling her into a hug, being mindful of the hot coffee she held. He kissed the top of her head. 'It will be our own little slice of paradise.'

'Edward! Edward!' A shrill voice cut through the peace of the morning.

'In here,' Edward called back. Carrie tried to wriggle out of his arms but he held her tight.

'It's Portia,' Carrie hissed.

'I know,' Edward said mildly, 'but we have nothing to hide. I've told Portia all about us.'

Carrie wasn't sure that Portia would be ready to see them in each other's arms but said nothing. It wasn't as if she wanted to pretend that nothing was going on, she just wasn't sure she was ready for how Portia might react.

Carrie could hear careful steps being taken as Portia navigated her no doubt expensive shoes around the rubble that had been left over from the roofers.

'Edward, there you are.' Carrie heard a sharp intake of breath and braced herself for what might come next.

'Good morning,' Portia added as Edward and Carrie swivelled their heads to look in her direction. Her tone was civil but her expression gave away her true feelings. Being told that Edward had moved on and seeing it were two different things.

'Morning, Portia. Would you like a coffee?' Edward asked as if he was unfazed by the situation.

'No, thank you. You make that ghastly instant stuff and you know how it gives me headaches.'

'I do. In that case I have some tea?'

'No, thank you. I came here to talk to

you before you start work but I can see that you are busy.'

'Not busy,' Edward said. 'In fact, quite the opposite. Carrie and I are just relaxing before a busy day but you are welcome to join us.'

'I see, but I need to speak to you privately.'

'I'll go and get breakfast sorted,' Carrie said, shrugging off Edward's arm and attempting to stand up but he held her back.

'Anything we need to talk about also affects Carrie, so Carrie is going to stay.'

Carrie thought she would rather be anywhere else than where she was in that moment. The idea of having to stay and listen to Edward and Portia talk about their relationship was something she didn't think she could bear.

'Since all we have left to talk about is your father's situation, it's not exactly private.'

Portia did not look happy. It was clear to Carrie that things were not turning out the way that she had planned, and for her own part she didn't really blame her.

'Fine,' Portia said crossing her arms. She looked around her as if she was expecting a chair to suddenly appear. Carrie saw this as her cue and got to her feet dragging Edward along with her.

'Why don't we go back to the caravan? We have chairs and a table set up outside and I expect we will all be more comfortable.'

Carrie also thought that she might be able to sneak away under the pretence of getting breakfast ready. It was true that the awkward situation was pretty much of Portia's making but that didn't mean that Carrie had to make it any worse.

Edward got to his feet but held on tightly to Carrie's hand and so they walked hand in hand back to the caravans with Portia following them, taking careful steps to avoid any dirt getting on the hem of her silk trousers.

When they reached Edward's caravan Carrie stepped inside and flipped the switch on the kettle. Looking through the window she could see that Barbara and Trevor's curtains were still closed. She wasn't sure whether their arrival would be a help or a hindrance to the horribly uncomfortable situation.

The kettle pinged and Carrie made two fresh cups of coffee and a cup of tea for Portia before carrying them back outside.

Portia and Edward were sitting at opposite ends of the table and looked like a couple about to get divorced. Carrie tried out a smile, which only Edward returned as she handed out the hot drinks.

'Anyone hungry?' Carrie asked when it was clear that no-one else was ready to speak.

'I think we're fine, Carrie, but thank you,' Edward said with a twinkle in his eye as if he had worked out her not so sneaky escape plan. He leaned back in his chair as Carrie sat down next to him.

'So, Portia, I take it this is about Charles?'

Portia took a sip of her tea and winced.

'As a matter of a fact it is.'

'How is he?' Edward said and now he leaned forward and Carrie could see how much he cared for the older man.

'Difficult to say. Some days are better than others.' Portia seemed to be struggling to hold in her emotion and once more Carrie felt sorry for her. Clearly she loved her father very much.

'I understand the doctors said that would be the case,' Edward said kindly.

'They did but on the good days it's hard not to get one's hopes up.'

'I know,' Edward said as Portia looked at him and they shared a moment. They might not agree on much but it was clear to Carrie that they both loved Charles.

'I came to talk to you because I have a proposition and I want you to hear me out before you say anything.' Since Portia seemed no longer able to look at

Edward, Carrie figured that whatever it was, Edward wasn't going to be too keen.

'I should start, I suppose, with an apology. I know that I behaved rather badly when I had my little fling.'

'For over a year,' Edward pointed out but he didn't sound angry just that he wanted the facts to be straight. Portia acknowledged that with a small nod.

'Well, I am sorry for any pain caused.'

'Portia, this is old ground. We've discussed this.

'We might care about each other but that doesn't mean that we have a future as a couple. The fact that you found someone else would suggest that you felt the same way, you just didn't know how to tell me.'

Portia looked off to the distance and Carrie saw her surreptitiously wipe a tear from her eye.

'I'm also aware that he is still in the picture,' Edward added mildly and Portia looked up sharply.

'How did you know . . . oh, never mind. It's only important that Daddy doesn't find out.' Portia said, flapping her hands with anxiety.

'Perhaps we could move this on to your proposal? I suspect our neighbours will be rising soon and then our audience will be bigger.'

'Fine. I will get straight to the point.' Portia said looking Edward in the eye. 'I want you to marry me.'

No More Time To Waste

Pardon?' Edward gasped and Carrie was a little relieved that he looked as shocked as she felt.

'Nothing grand, just a small simple ceremony at the manor. Somewhere Daddy can easily get to without much travelling.'

'I heard what you said, Portia, I wasn't asking for specific arrangements.'

'We can get divorced as soon as, well after Daddy has . . . ' She couldn't seem to finish that sentence. 'Assuming you want to, or we could stay married and see how it goes.' Portia kept talking as if she hadn't heard what Edward had said.

Carrie blinked and thought about pinching herself. Surely this was some kind of surreal nightmare.

'You know that Daddy wants me to be happy and settled, which for his generation is all about getting married.'

'I do,' Edward conceded, 'but I also know that he would want you to be serious about marrying someone.'

'Maybe I am serious,' Portia said but she didn't seem able to look Edward in the eye.

'Portia, whilst we may be fond of each other, we aren't in love.'

Portia opened her mouth to argue but Edward held up a hand. 'With each other,' he added.

'But I can't marry him!' Portia wailed and Edward leaned back in his seat, almost as if he was afraid Portia was going to explode. Edward looked helplessly at Carrie. Carrie shifted her seat so that she was closer to Portia and took a deep breath.

'This other man, you love him?' Carrie asked as gently as she could.

'I do,' Portia said, looking surprised as if she had only just realised that Carrie was present.

'Is he married?' Carrie asked, again as gently as she could.

'No! Gary's not married!' Portia shouted, looking scandalised at the very idea.

'Right,' Carrie said, 'then why can't you marry him? Is he a priest?' The thought just struck Carrie and her heart sank. That really would be a problem.

'Worse. He's a plumber.' Portia dissolved into heart felt sobs.

Carrie patted Portia awkwardly on the arm but she had to admit that she didn't really understand what was going on and then a lightbulb went on in her head.

'Ah, you think your dad won't approve?' Edward was staring with his mouth open. 'Portia, you can't be serious about this?'

*　*　*

'Charles just wants you to be happy.'

'I know he does,' Portia's voice shuddered with sobs, 'but Daddy would never let me marry someone who has a trade.'

Edward laughed and Carrie glared at

236

him. Edward made an effort to stop laughing but a smile still played at the edges of his mouth.

'Portia, I'm sure that Gary makes way more money than I do. And admittedly he doesn't have a title, but he also won't inherit an estate that barely makes ends meet.'

'Well, he does have his own five-bedroom house on that new estate just outside of town,' Portia conceded with a sniff.

'I'm sure Charles would prefer you to live there than here with me in a humble cottage. And I know he wants you to marry for love.'

'But he loves you,' Portia said.

'He does and so I know that he wouldn't want either of us to be unhappy in some sort of pseudo marriage put on for his benefit only.'

'Gary does treat me like a princess,' Portia said, giving Edward a hard stare. It was clear to Carrie that Edward had never treated Portia like a princess and she had to hide her grin. 'He's even asked me but I told him I couldn't.' Portia's bottom lip started to wobble again.

'Right,' Carrie said, feeling it was time to take charge of things. 'Edward, Portia, I think it's time we went to see your father.'

'I can't,' Portia said, sounding panicked. 'What if he says no?'

'Then at least you'll know but I have a feeling he is going to say yes,' Carrie said, picking up the Jeep keys from the caravan and throwing them to Edward. 'Edward, you're driving.'

Carrie sat in the back seat and gawped as Edward pulled the truck up outside some giant wooden security gates. The gates slid open and Edward slowly drove up the winding drive way to a modern house that looked about the same size as the manor house. Carrie hoped that she wasn't wrong to suggest that Portia speak to her dad.

Clearly in Portia's family wealth and status were important. A man in a suit stepped out of the front door and down the stone steps before opening the car door for Portia.

'Miss Portia,' he said with a small bow.

Carrie climbed out of the car before the man could hold the door for her. She always felt uncomfortable around that sort of behaviour. Portia led them up the steps and into a triple height hallway, complete with chandeliers and huge portraits.

'Your father is in the orangery,' the man said, appearing behind them and closing the door.

'Thank you, Carter,' Portia said, walking off with Edward and Carrie bringing up the rear. Carrie pulled a wide-eyed expression at Edward, who just smiled and shrugged. He was clearly used to it.

Portia led them through the grand house and then opened a door in to a room that was made mainly of glass. Charles was sitting in a leather armchair reading a newspaper and drinking a cup of tea. He looked frail but his eyes were bright.

'Portia, darling, so lovely to see you.' He reached out a hand to Portia. 'And I see you have brought Edward and a friend.'

Carrie hung back, feeling somewhat awkward, not sure how she would be introduced. As Edward's girlfriend? She couldn't see that happening. Edward walked over and firmly shook Charles's hand.

'This is Carrie,' Edward said with a smile and gestured Carrie to come over. Carrie had an overwhelming urge to curtsey but managed to stop herself.

'Carrie, my dear, lovely to meet you,' Charles said with a warm smile.

'You are not my first visitor today, Portia. I appear to have become very popular all of a sudden.'

'Really?' Portia said, sounding distracted as if she was trying to work out how to break the news to her father.

'Yes, a handsome devil by the name of Gary.'

Portia, Edward and Carrie seemed to

all freeze at precisely the same moment.

'Gary came to see you?' Portia managed to squeak out.

'He did,' Charles said rather solemnly and Carrie blanched. This really had been a huge mistake. Charles was about to break Portia's heart.

'And I have one question for you, my dear.'

'Yes, Daddy?'

'Why did you turn him down?'

Portia opened her mouth and Carrie was sure she had been preparing some kind of defence but on the words sinking in, her face crumpled and she started to cry.

'Oh, my darling,' Charles said, opening his arms and Portia knelt beside his chair and dissolved into his hug. 'How could you think that I would turn down any suitor who truly loves you? My silly girl.' Charles rubbed at Portia's back. 'How could you believe that I thought you and Edward should get married?'

Edward stared open-mouthed and

Portia wriggled out of her hug.

'You're a fine man, Edward, but you were never right for my Portia. No offence meant, of course.'

'None taken, sir,' Edward answered with a grin.

'Why didn't you say anything?' Portia asked as her father wiped away her tears.

'Because I don't like to meddle in my grown-up children's lives and I couldn't bring myself to tell you that I didn't think it was the right thing for either of you.'

'I thought it would make you happy.'

Charles shook his head.

'The only thing that I need to be happy is to know that you are happy. Do you love Gary?'

'Yes, Daddy,' Portia said and her face broke into the kind of smile that Carrie thought only really happens when love is involved.

'Then you'd best go find him and tell him. I told him he had my blessing, but that it was entirely your decision.'

Edward looked at Carrie and held

out his hand, which she took. They smiled at each other. Nothing would keep them apart, not that anything ever could.

But without words it was clear that they were both pleased that Portia would also get her happy ever after.

'Why not get Carter to bring round the car?' Charles said, kissing his daughter on the cheek. 'And when you have found Gary, I expect you to invite him here for supper. I'd like to get to know my son-in-law to be.

Portia kissed her father, then kissed Edward on the cheek before pulling Carrie into a tight hug. Carrie was a little startled but hugged Portia back. Then Portia ran from the room.

'Well that's my Portia sorted, now what about you two?'

Edward grinned and Carrie looked a little shocked that they had been assessed so quickly.

'Carrie and I haven't really spoken about what's next. It's all been a bit complicated.'

'That's life, son, but take some advice from an old man. If you know, you know — so don't waste any more time.'

'We won't,' Edward said shaking the older man's hand.

'Anyone can see that she is perfect for you, lad. Don't let her get away,' Charles whispered, although Carrie could hear every word. Edward nodded and turned to Carrie.

'It was very nice to meet you,' Carrie said as Edward took her hand.

'And you,' Charles said with a smile that made his eyes sparkle.

Edward and Carrie walked out of the grand house hand in hand and climbed into Edward's jeep.

'Well, that was a good call,' Edward said as they drove down the drive.

'I have to admit I was worried for a moment there that Charles would say no.'

'I can't believe that the mess has finally been sorted out and everyone seems to be happy. It's such a relief.'

Carrie nodded and they drove in

comfortable silence.

'You are happy, Carrie, aren't you?' Edward asked.

'More than I thought possible,' Carrie said, turning her attention from the view out of the window and back to Edward. Edward took one hand off the steering wheel and reached out a hand for hers.

'Me too,' he said. 'Me too.'

Home At Last

Edward drove them back to the lane near the cottage and they walked hand in hand through the woods.

It was a hive of activity with volunteers all over the site painting wooden front doors and window frames and making paths to the front doors.

Edward stopped to speak to a couple and Carrie slipped away to her cottage. It was quiet inside.

The whitewash on the walls had been finished and was now drying out. She walked on through and took up her usual spot on the back step.

'I knew I would find my happiness here,' she whispered. 'I knew it.'

She looked up to the sky and smiled.

'Thank you,' she said softly and her mind's eye conjured up a picture of her grandparents working in their back garden, their little slice of heaven as they had called it.

She imagined they were smiling at her as if they had always known that she would come back.

A shadow crossed her path and she could see Edward standing over her.

'Talking to yourself?' he asked with a gentle smile that told Carrie he knew exactly who she was talking to.

'I feel so close to them here,' she said with a shrug. 'When I came here, it was the strangest thing. I'd never been here before but I felt like it was my home.'

'I know the feeling,' Edward said as he knelt down in front of her.

'Carrie, there is something I wanted to ask you. I've been waiting for everything to get sorted out and now that it is, I don't think I need to wait any more.'

Carrie felt her pulse quicken and she was almost too scared to look at Edward. She felt a hand under her chin and he tilted her face so that he could look her in the eye.

'Will you marry me?'

Carrie blinked and felt like all the air had been squeezed from her lungs, leaving her unable to speak.

Edward pulled a small velvet box from his pocket and opened it, holding it out in front of him.

'I wanted to get the biggest diamond I could find but Barbara said you were more of a silver patterned woman.'

Edward took the ring out of the box and picked up Carrie's left hand. He waited, as if he knew that she needed the time.

'I love you, Carrie. I know I made a complete hash of everything and that you might need some time to think about it but I know that you are my true love and that I want to be with you for ever.'

Edward waited as Carrie looked from the ring to Edward's face and back again.

'I understand if you aren't ready to decide yet. So you don't need to worry or feel pressured into anything . . . '

'Shut up, Edward,' Carrie said,

frowning. That wasn't exactly what she meant to say, so she leaned forward and kissed him. Edward wrapped his arms around Carrie and lost his balance, so they found themselves lying on their backs looking up at the sky and laughing.

'Is that a yes?' Edward said when Carrie managed to stop laughing enough to speak.

'That's a definite yes. I love you, Edward. I want to be with you for ever, too.'

Edward levered himself up on his elbow and took Carrie's left hand in his and slipped the ring on to her finger. Carrie held her hand up to the light.

'Do you like it? If not, I can go and get you one with big diamonds.'

Edward looked genuinely concerned and so Carrie reached over and kissed him again.

'I love it. It's absolutely perfect.'

'Edward!' The shout and voice was distinctive and Edward shook his head.

'We should probably go and see what that is all about.'

'We should — and we have some people to tell, I think.'

Edward grinned, got to his feet and helped Carrie to hers. With one arm wrapped around her shoulder Edward guided Carrie back through the cottage.

Portia was there, as they knew she would be, but this time she was holding hands tightly with a broad, tall man who was grinning from ear to ear.

Portia turned in their direction and she rushed over, dragging Gary with her.

'Edward, Carrie, darlings. Gary and I are getting married!' Portia announced.

The volunteers who had gathered to see what all the fuss was about clapped and cheered as Portia flashed the biggest diamond that Carrie had ever seen.

'Portia, that's wonderful,' Edward said, stepping forward to kiss Portia on the cheek and then to shake hands with Gary.

Portia pulled Carrie in to a hug.

'I'm sorry about our little misunderstanding. Friends?' Portia whispered.

'Friends,' Carrie said with a smile.

'Carrie and I have some news of our own,' Edward said loudly enough so that the small crowd of volunteers could hear what he had to say.

'I have asked Carrie if she would do me the honour of being my wife and she has said yes.'

Portia threw her arms around Edward as another wave of cheers and clapping started. There was squealing too and Carrie felt herself pulled into a bear hug with Barbara and Trevor.

'Oh, how wonderful!' Barbara exclaimed.

'It can't be a surprise,' Carrie said, feeling as though her face was starting to ache from all the smiling, as if the happiness was getting ready to burst out of her, 'you helped Edward pick the ring.'

'I did, but I had no idea what you would say.'

'I love him, Barbara, with all my heart.'

'That's what I was hoping you would say,' Barbara said as she pulled Carrie into another hug, 'and I know you will be very happy together.'

'We will,' Edward said, reappearing beside Carrie and drawing her into his arms.

'And where are you going to live?' Barbara asked with a mischievous air.

'Right here, of course,' Edward said, 'in our very own slice of paradise.'

Carrie looked up at him.

'Are you sure?'

'I've never been more sure in my life. Without this place I would never have met you and besides, it's a place we both call home.'

'Home,' Carrie said before reaching up to kiss Edward once more.

We do hope that you have enjoyed reading this large print book.

Did you know that all of our titles are available for purchase?

We publish a wide range of high quality large print books including:
Romances, Mysteries, Classics
General Fiction
Non Fiction and Westerns

Special interest titles available in large print are:
The Little Oxford Dictionary
Music Book, Song Book
Hymn Book, Service Book

Also available from us courtesy of Oxford University Press:
Young Readers' Dictionary
(large print edition)
Young Readers' Thesaurus
(large print edition)

For further information or a free brochure, please contact us at:
Ulverscroft Large Print Books Ltd.,
The Green, Bradgate Road, Anstey,
Leicester, LE7 7FU, England.
Tel: (00 44) **0116 236 4325**
Fax: (00 44) **0116 234 0205**

Budding criminologist Ellie is glad to help her gran recuperate after an accident, expecting to spend a quiet month in rural Wales before heading back to London to submit her PhD. But she's bemused to find that she's something of a celebrity in the village, and expected to help solve a series of devastating livestock thefts for which there is no shortage of suspects. She's also wrong-footed by the friendly overtures of handsome young farmer Tom — even though a relationship is absolutely the last thing she wants or needs . . .

JEMIMA'S NOBLEMAN

Anne Holman

1816: When her father's famous fan shop in the Strand is reduced to ashes, Jemima dons the clothing of a maid and moves with him to the docklands of London — and is present at an accident where William, Earl of Swanington, almost literally falls into her lap! But William is fleeing from accusations that he's murdered a servant — and when he sees the beautiful Jemima at a Society ball, he wonders if she's the one who robbed him after his accident! Can true love blossom in such circumstances?

CHRISTMAS DOWN UNDER

Alan C. Williams

Australia, 1969: Manchester lass Pamela has given life in Sydney as a Ten Pound Pom a fair go, but since her husband ran off with a younger woman, she longs to return to the UK. However, when she books a one-way flight to take herself and her four-year-old daughter Sharon home by Christmas, it appears fate has other ideas. As Pamela's festive project at work takes off and she meets gorgeous but fashion-challenged teacher Nick, she begins to wonder whether life in Australia has more to offer than she'd thought . . .

CHRISTMAS GHOSTS AT THE PRIORY

Fenella J Miller

Miss Eloise Granville is begrudgingly accepting of her arranged marriage to Viscount Garrick Forsythe — but when she discovers he is not aware of her infirmity, she is horrified. The wedding is only three weeks away, and it's far too late to cancel. Will he think he has been tricked? As Eloise anxiously awaits Garrick's arrival at St Cuthbert's Priory, the resident ghosts learn of the betrothal and unleash a fury that puts them both in grave danger. Will they find love amidst the chaos, or will circumstances push them apart?

THE RAGS OF TIME

Pamela Kavanagh

Escaping an emotionally unbearable life with her husband, Hannah flees with her young daughter to the town of Malpas, where she hopes to uncover her family's past and build a new life. Arriving with no wedding ring and baby Vinnie tucked under her shawl, Hannah struggles to find a place to stay. As nightfall approaches, she stumbles across a cottage owned by kindly Widow Nightingale, who takes them in — but will Hannah be able to find work, build a stable life for her daughter, and discover happiness in the town?